A
Celebration
Book Club Selection

South & North, East & West

edited by Michael Rosen

Given By   Pritchett-Tripp PTO

To   Pritchett School

Date   August 1993

Commemoration

Welcome to school.
Dist. 102 4th Grade Class of 1993-94.

South and North East and West

Illustrations on pages 1, 2, 3, 92 and 96 by Charlotte Voake
Lettering on pages 1 and 3 by Jovica Veljović

First U.S. edition 1992
First published in Great Britain in 1992 by Walker Books Ltd., London.

Library of Congress Catalog Card Number 91-58749
Library of Congress Cataloging-in-Publication Data.
South and north, east and west: the Oxfam anthology of children's stories/
edited by Michael Rosen with an introduction by Whoopi Goldberg. 1st U.S. edition
Summary: a collection of twenty-five traditional tales from countries around the world,
including Iran, Brazil, and Greece.
ISBN 1-56402-117-3
1. Tales, [1. Folklore.] I. Rosen, Michael, 1946-
PZ8. 1.S707 1992
398.2–dc20   91-58749

10 9 8 7 6 5 4 3 2 1

Printed in and bound in Italy by
Arnoldo Mondadori Editore, Verona

Candlewick Press
2067 Massachusetts Avenue
Cambridge, Massachusetts 02140

THE OXFAM BOOK OF CHILDREN'S STORIES

South and North, East and West

EDITED BY MICHAEL ROSEN

CANDLEWICK PRESS
CAMBRIDGE, MASSACHUSETTS

CONTENTS

INTRODUCTION

Illustrated by Nicola Bayley

When I first started acting, I used to become lots of different characters on stage and I'd try to tell their stories. And I really learned from those people. I didn't just become them to look at—I understood them, because I'd told their stories and I'd heard them too.

Often, when we meet people, we see only what they look like from the outside. We only understand what they're like on the inside when we listen to their stories, and we're usually surprised to find how much we have in common.

Stories are special because, in a way, they are very safe. You can hear them and learn about things that would frighten you if you had to face them for the first time in your own life. Some of the stories in this book are from countries you may hardly know, places that may seem a little scary. But when you've heard their stories, you won't feel the same way. You'll feel closer to your brothers and sisters around the world. You'll feel part of the whole world rather than far away from the countries in the book.

Often these stories have many things in common with the stories you've grown up with. Sometimes though, they are not the same at all. A good example is the story about the first people on earth who came out of an enormous bee sting on the knee of Ngutapa. The people who tell that story live in the Brazilian rain forest and want to protect their forest forever. They feel that their natural world is sacred. Perhaps we should feel more that way too.

The stories in this book are told by people Oxfam works with. Many of them are children. Oxfam is an organization that helps people who are poor grow more food to eat or earn more money to live on. But even though these people are poor, their stories are very rich. I hope they'll encourage you to listen more for the stories that are all around you. It's the best way to really understand *your* whole world.

Whoopi Goldberg

THE MAN WHO GAVE PEOPLE THINGS TO LOOK AFTER

illustrated by Axel Scheffler

Once there was a little old man walking along the road with a walking stick. Soon he came to a house and knocked on the door with the stick, *tratt, tratt, tratt.*

A woman came out and he said to her, "Good woman, would you be so kind as to look after my walking stick? Now, don't go burning it in your stove, will you? I'll be back for it in the morning."

And so he went on his way.

Later that day the woman was baking some bread in her stove, and this stove didn't run on electricity or gas—it burned wood. Well, she

was running out of wood and, as she picked up the last bits and pieces off her woodpile, she picked up the little old man's walking stick. Without a wink or a blink, she poked it into the stove, *pook, pook, pook.*

Next day the little old man was back. "Where's my walking stick?" he said.

"Oh, dear me," said the woman, "I must have burnt it. Now, don't you worry yourself. I'll get you a new one just as soon as ever."

"Oh, no," said the little old man. "Oh, no. You burnt my stick in your stove, so I'll have your stove, indeed I will."

And with no please or thank you, he picked up

9

the woman's little clay stove and hurried off with it.

Soon he came to a woman who was looking after some goats, and he said to her, "Good woman, would you be so kind as to look after my stove for me? Now, don't go letting your goats trample on it, or it'll break. I'll be back for it in the morning."

And so he went on his way.

Later that day the woman fell asleep under a tree and while she lay there, not knowing a wit or a twit, two of her goats trampled on the little clay stove and broke it up, *crack, crick, crock.*

Next day the little old man was back.

"Where's my stove?" he said.

"Oh, dear me," said the woman, "my goats must have trampled on it. Now, don't you worry yourself. I'll get you a new one just as soon as ever."

"Oh, no," said the little old man. "Oh, no. Your goats broke my stove, so I'll have your goats, indeed I will."

And with no please or thank you, he grabbed the woman's goats and hurried off with them.

Soon he came to a house where the people were having a wedding feast, and he said to the bridegroom, "Good man, would you be so kind as to look after my goats for me? Now, don't you and your new wife go eating them for your feast. I'll be back for them in the morning."

And so he went on his way.

Later that day the wedding feast was in full swing, and they ran out of food. No one likes to run out of food at a wedding, and it wasn't long before the guests were sitting down to eat roast goat, *chobble, chobble, chobble.*

Next day the little old man was back.

"Where are my goats?" he said.

"Oh, dear me," said the bridegroom, "we must have eaten them. Now, don't you worry yourself. I'll get you some more just as soon as ever."

"Oh, no," said the little old man. "Oh,

no. You and your wife ate my goats, so I'll have your wife, indeed I will."

And with no please or thank you, he grabbed the bride and hurried off with her. Further down the road he popped her into a sack and tied up the top.

Soon he came to the house of an old, old woman.

He knocked on the door, *tratt, tratt, tratt,* and when the old, old woman came out, he said, "Good woman, would you be so kind as to look after my sack for me? Now, don't you go opening it, and I'll be back for it in the morning."

And he went on his way.

Later that day the old, old woman heard a noise from the sack, *ayee, ayee, ayee,* so she opened it, and out came the wife.

"Oh, no, did you ever!" cried the old, old woman. "Now, listen, girl, away with you! Hurry! Get away from here just as fast as your legs will take you."

Away ran the wife into the forest, and the old, old woman was not long following

her. There she hunted out snakes, seized them, and stuffed them into the sack, *sleess, sleess, sleess.*

Next day the little old man was back.

"Where's my sack?" he said.

"Right here where you left it, old feller," said she.

"You're a good woman, indeed you are," he said, and he put the sack on his back and he was away out the door, down the road, and into the forest. Once he was deep, deep among the trees, he sat himself down and began opening the sack with his knife, *kwerk, kwork, kwerk.* But the moment the hole was big enough, out came the snakes. They slithered all over him and bit him more times than you could count, and that was the end of the little old man.

FOX, ALLIGATOR, AND RABBIT

illustrated by Louise Voce

Once there was a fast, wide river. On one side stood a market and on the other a town. So to get to the market from the town, you had to cross the river. But—and this was a mighty big "but"—in the middle of the river was Alligator. Now, alligators have their own special way of letting you know they're around—they try and eat you.

One day Fox and Rabbit wanted to cross the river to the market. Rabbit was working on some kind of a plan.

"Say, Fox," he says, "is it true you foxes are known for being just about the smartest, cleverest creatures around?"

"Yep," says Fox.

"Then hows about you taking me across the river?"

"Sure," says Fox, "I'll do it for some of those melons you got there."

"That's fine," says Rabbit.

"Then you just watch me, Rabbit," says Fox, "and you'll see how to lick this alligator thing, no problem."

So Fox hightails it out into the river, and you can be sure he knows some things that no one else knows. He knows that Alligator likes his porridge so hot it'd burn your eyelashes to eat it. And another thing—Alligator is stupid. He is so stupid, he's been known to think his tail was a fish and give himself a terrible bite. *WHEEEEE*, that hurt!

So Fox is swimming along and he meets Alligator. One more thing about Alligator—he may be stupid, but believe me, he *thinks* he's one smart guy.

Fox gives him something like this: "Say, Alligator, if I can come home with you and have a bite or two to eat with you, would you let me across this river?"

And something else about Alligator. He just loves to give people some of his roasting hot porridge and then sit back and watch them burn their mouths out—*HOWOWEEE!*

So you know what Alligator says when Fox invites himself around to Alligator's place…? "Sure—but I'll cook—and it'll be porridge."

And Alligator can hardly stop himself from laughing, thinking about Fox's tongue hitting that hot porridge.

As soon as they get to Alligator's place, Alligator starts cooking the porridge. About two hours later, it's ready and he pours it out into a big, big bowl to eat.

Fox takes his spoon down to the porridge real slow, he lifts it up to his mouth just as slow, and then as soon as it hits his tongue he says, "Oooh, no, this is much too cold for me, Alligator. Why not put it out in the sun to warm up, huh?"

Alligator loves that. Make it even hotter. Great idea. Then it'll be so hot, Fox won't even be able to bear looking at it. He won't be crossing the river today, thinks Alligator, and he puts the porridge out in the sun.

Two hours later he brings it back in.

"Try that, Fox," says Alligator. He can hardly wait for the screams.

Down goes the spoon real slow, up it comes just as slow, and then as soon as it hits Fox's tongue, he says, "Oooh, no, it's still too cold. Put it out in the sun for a while more."

So out goes the porridge again for three hours more. "This porridge is going to be awful hot," thinks Alligator. "Even I might find it tough getting it down me."

After all this time, the porridge is stone cold.

"I'll give it a try now," says Fox. "I just hope it's hotted up some."

Down goes the spoon real slow, up it comes just as slow, and as soon as it hits Fox's tongue he says, "Hey, Alligator, now we are really cooking on all four burners. This is what I call hot. Just give me that

13

porridge." And Fox digs into that porridge like there's no tomorrow.

Believe me, Alligator is impressed. He's sitting there figuring and figuring about how Fox's mouth can take all that burning.

With Fox finished, Alligator says to him, "If you like it that much, Brother, why not have some more?"

"I sure would like to," says Fox, "but I've got business at the market today. I've got to stock up on porridge."

And now Alligator says, "OK. I'll let you get across. It's been a pleasure to see someone like my porridge so much."

"The pleasure's mine," says Fox, and off he swims.

And as he's swimming along, Fox is thinking of those melons Rabbit has promised him. But Alligator's sitting there eating the cold porridge and he's figuring and figuring: "How come my porridge is so cold, but his porridge was so hot? Now, that's something I must ask that Fox."

So quick as a fish Alligator swims after Fox, and in two blinks of an eye he's up to him.

"Say, Fox, tell me this. How come your porridge was hotter than mine?"

"Sheesh," thinks Fox, "he's figured it out. I'd better get these legs moving."

"What's that you say?" says Fox.
"How come your porridge—"
"My what?" says Fox.
"Your porridge."
"My pocket?"
"No, your porridge."
"What about my porridge?"

"How come it was hotter than mine?"

But by now, Fox has made it to the other side, and has climbed out onto the bank.

"I'll tell you tomorrow," says Fox, and he's off to the market.

When he gets there, what do you know—Rabbit's standing there waiting for him.

"OK, big boy," says Fox, "how come you got across?"

And Rabbit says, "You're not the only one with a little sense around here. What do you think I was doing while you were with Alligator?"

At that, he slaps his sides and whoops with laughter.

Fox watches him for a while and then says, kind of slow and soft, "So tell me this, Rabbit. If you weren't watching me to see how I got across just then…how are you going to get back?"

Rabbit stops all his laughing right there and then.

15

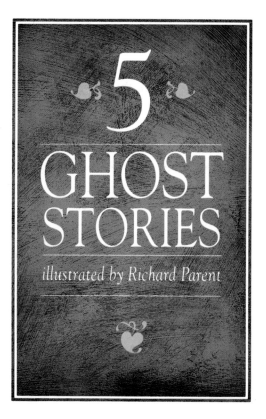

THE HOOK

It was a dark night, and John was walking along an old country road. He was tired, and the rain was beating down on his face. Where would he spend the night? He couldn't sleep out here in the rain, and the ground was sodden. On he walked. Again and again, he lifted his head into the rain and tried to make out the shape of a hut or a house. Nothing. But then, after what seemed hours, he noticed a dark hump by the side of the road that could be a house. And, indeed, the closer he walked, the more it took on the shape of a house. But at the same time, the nearer he stepped, the more strange and forbidding it seemed. High, dark, no lights.

He heard his feet on the stone path, and after a moment's pause, he pounded on the door with his hand. Nothing happened. He pounded again. A light came on in the window above and then followed the sound of feet on the stairs. The bolts banged back, one at the top, one at the bottom, and the key turned in the lock. When the door opened, John could make out a great slab of a man.

"What do you want?" he said.

"I seem to have lost my way," said John, "and I would be most obliged if you'd let me have a place to lie down for the night."

16

"Well, you've found the right place here," said the man. "This is an inn."

John felt a warm wave travel down his back, and he saw himself passing through the luxuries of a hot bath, soft towels, hot soup, a roaring fire, a soft bed.

"Step right in," said the man.

John could have hugged him.

And indeed, it was just as he had imagined: the bath, the towels, the soup, the fire, and the bed.

Just before he settled down for the night, John looked around the room. He caught sight of himself in the mirror, his eyes dark and tired. He draped his clothes over a chair, hung his old rucksack on a hook on the wall, and fell asleep before he knew it.

A couple of hours later, he woke up.

The room was pitch black. He scarcely knew he had opened his eyes. He lay there for a moment wondering why he had woken up—then slowly he realized he could smell smoke. He sniffed the cold air. That was most definitely smoke. John lay in his bed staring into the blackness. "Smoke…smoke…" He said the word over in his mind, not thinking about what it really meant until quite suddenly it joined another word—*fire*. Fire? He felt gripped with a terror.

"Where am I? Where is the fire? Above me, below me, alongside me? How will I get out?" And yet, though his mind ran wild, his body lay still. He couldn't move. Then he heard the rushing of feet outside his room, muffled shouts, a cry in the distance. It was then that he realized his body was so overcome with tiredness from the day before that it wouldn't move until he told it to.

"Move!" And now the legs kicked the blankets off, the arms grabbed the clothes, the hands seized the door handle, and the feet took him out of the door. Someone dashed past him in the passage and he saw flames curling out of a doorway. He turned and ran to the stairs.

But where there had been stairs before, there was now a pool of white smoke. Right next to his ear, a flaming beam roared down into the pool of smoke, followed by a sickening scream. He looked back, and the flames that curled out of the doorway were now reaching toward him. He had no choice—jump or be burned alive. But jump into what? John asked himself no more questions, covered his face with his shirt, and leapt into the pool of white smoke.

He landed on a burning banister, jumped off before it could burn him and, on looking up, saw a dark hole. Without knowing why, he jumped for it, dived into it, lunging through it. Only then did he realize how wise a move he had made. That dark hole was the night, visible for a brief moment when a door fell to the floor. John looked at himself. He was outside the inn, standing in the courtyard in his nightshirt, looking up at the blazing building.

A wall of flame stood between him and the room he had just leapt from. Upstairs was a furnace, sparks rising into the night air like fireworks. He turned away and ran, only now realizing what a horrible death he had just avoided. He ran down the road he had walked earlier that night. "There must be another house nearby," he thought, and he ran on faster than he had ever run before.

A house came into view. He ran to the door and slammed the knocker against it again and again.

He screamed out, "The inn's on fire. The inn down the road's on fire. People are dying. Help! Help!"

Someone stuck his head out of the window above him, "What's going on? What the devil do you think you're doing?"

"Can't you hear me?" shouted John. "The inn's on fire. People are dying. Get out of bed and help."

The voice above said, "Hold your horses, man. What are you talking about?

There's no inn up the road. We're the only house this side of the moor till you get to the sea."

"For God's sake, believe me. I know what I'm saying. I was there, just now. I've just come from there. I was asleep … I was …"

His voice faded.

One way or another he managed to persuade the man of the house and his brother to come with him up the road. But no matter where they looked there was no inn, no fire, no smoke, no ashes. Nothing. Well, not exactly nothing.

Beside the road, in a place where an inn might once have stood, was an old ruin. By now, it was dawn, the sky was growing lighter and they could see the old mossy stones lying in heaps, the broken walls leaning against trees, as if looking for help.

John ran amongst them. He was beginning to feel bewildered and anxious. The layout of the rooms seemed the same as the inn. There was the back door, the little lobby, the back room, and yes, there were a few of the steps up to the first floor, which would mean—his eyes were flicking to and fro with the excitement of it now— which would mean that just up there, along that wall, yes, that would have been the room he slept in. But it was impossible. This was the ruin of a house that must have been standing here over a hundred years ago.

And then he saw it. Something up on the wall that made his whole body freeze. There, next to the place where his bed might have been, was a hook. And on the hook was … his rucksack.

18

TEETH

It is about twelve o'clock at night, and the old feller Hedley is out for a walk. He reach into his pocket and take out a cigarette. He reach again into the same pocket—but no matches. He feel all round his pockets, but it is the same for all. No matches. He look around wondering, is there someone round here who can give me a light?

There is no one in sight, so he stroll on down the road. Before long, he see a tall man walking toward him.

When he get near enough, Hedley lean toward him, saying, "Excuse me, have you got a light?"

At that, the man smile—and I tell you the truth, it is the smile of a ghost: long and slow, showing the longest set of teeth Hedley ever see in all his long life.

Hedley scream, Lord he scream. He turn and then run back up the road he just been walking down. He run so quick, you hardly see his legs. Now his breath coming hard, and he slow down till he get to another man.

"Man, I glad to see you. At the other end of the road, I see this ghost with really long teeth and I tell no lie, he smile."

But as he say this, the man smile. And Lord, it's the same smile, long and slow, showing the longest set of teeth that Hedley ever see.

What can he do, poor Hedley? He scream, turn, and run back up the road the way he go the first time. Once again he see a man coming. But this time, he sure it not the ghost. This is a man, a living, son of a mother, man.

"Oh, man, I glad to see you. I just see a ghost and—"

And the man say, "Ever see teeth like these?" And Lord, it's the same smile, long and slow, showing the longest set of teeth that old Hedley ever see.

Now poor Hedley, he not know what to do, where to go or nothing. But turn around he go, screaming for the Lord, back down the road again. And once again there is a man coming toward him. Hedley screaming, but he still have the cigarette in his hand.

So the man see him coming, and he laugh and say, "What happen, Hedley? You want light for your cigarette?"

Now, Hedley, he can't stand it no more. He think, "I stand up to this ghost this time, except he's not a ghost this time."

So Hedley say to the man, "Look now, ever seen teeth as long as these?"

And he pull back his lips to show his teeth…

And the man answer him, "Yeah."

"Where?" say Hedley.

"That man behind you," say the man.

Hedley turn and see the ghost once more.

"Ahhhhh!"

He scream louder than ever and run off the road into the forest, on and on all the way to Cockpit County, and he never, never, never seen again.

THE CLIFF

Anthony was on holiday in Malta visiting his grandparents. He was only three, looking out of the window of their car, seeing places he had never seen before. Slowly, he started feeling unhappy. He didn't know why. He just knew that the mood in the car had changed, and Mom and Dad and Grandad weren't singing and laughing anymore. Grandad was looking to and fro like he didn't know where he was. Mom had stopped talking and was watching Grandad and glancing across at Dad with funny looks.

Anthony started crying. He got slapped. That started Mom and Dad shouting. Anthony cried even louder. Grandad was shaking his head. Then someone dared say the word. *Lost.* Everyone looked out of the window so that no one would have to look at anyone else and see a face as scared as their own.

They were in a dark alley, with rocks on either side of them and old olive trees and vines hanging over the track. Anthony wailed, "We lost, we lost."

His mother was thinking they hadn't brought enough to drink.

Just then, up in front of them, the figure of a woman in a long dark dress

with a shawl around her shoulders, waved at the car.

"God bless the good woman," said Anthony's mother. "She'll help us."

But as the car reached her, she seemed to slip from sight.

"Where is she now?" shouted Dad.

"I don't know. I was just looking for the water bottle," said Mom.

"I was checking the gas," said Grandad. "What were *you* doing?"

"I was... I was... watching her and she just—flip—" (Dad snapped his fingers) "—and she was gone. I must have blinked."

Grandad stopped the car.

"She can't have gone far. I'll go and see."

"I'll come too," said Dad.

The two men climbed out of the car and looked around. She wasn't on the right side; she wasn't on the left side.

"We'll just walk on a little and see if she's run ahead," said Grandad.

The track twisted around the rocks and trees, and in just a few strides the two men disappeared from sight.

Mom sat in the car and waited with Anthony. No more than a few breaths after the men had gone from view, Anthony started wailing again.

"Where Daddy? Where Daddy?"

The same thought was going through his mother's mind. She didn't like the way the trees scraped the roof of the car. She suddenly felt very alone.

"But this is ridiculous," she thought. "They've only gone around the corner. If this was a straight open road, they would be scarcely a few feet away."

But she didn't like it. Maybe she should get out of the car and look for them. She wouldn't be a moment. Anthony would be all right in his car seat, just so that she could keep the two men in her sight. So she got up to go.

"Now, listen, Anthony, I'm just going to stand over there by that tree so that I can see Daddy and Grandad."

Anthony let out another horrible wail.

"Don't go, Mommmeee. Don't go."

Just then, Dad and Grandad appeared. All the color had gone from their faces. They climbed into the car, breathing deeply, not saying a word.

Grandad was shaking his head again and again. Dad was letting his breath out through his teeth.

"Well?" said Mother. "Did you see her?" half hoping they wouldn't tell her.

"No, no, it's not that," said Grandad.

"Well, what?"

"Just around that corner is the highest cliff in Malta. And as sure as night follows day, if we'd driven on, we'd have shot over the top, down into the sea."

THE DAUGHTER

The taxi driver had finished his day's work. He was hot and tired, but there was not long to go now…soon be home. It was dark, and people were in their houses eating. Ahead of him on the road, someone was pedaling along on his bike. It was raining. The old taxi jogged along. It was then he noticed a young girl standing under a tree by the side of the road some way ahead. "It was quite a long way to the next village—perhaps she could do with a lift," thought the taxi driver.

He brought the taxi to a stop next to the tree.

"Do you want a lift?" he asked.

"Thank you, mister," said the girl.

"I'll take you home," said the taxi driver. "Where do you live?"

"I can't pay," said the girl, "I've got no money."

"Don't worry, it's been a good day for me. Plenty of business. I'll take you home for nothing."

"I live in the house on that hill, just up the road there."

"OK, let's go," said the taxi driver.

The taxi jogged on till they came to the hill. When they reached the house, the taxi driver knocked on the door and an old woman came out.

"I've brought your daughter home," said the taxi driver, "she was—"

"What are you talking about, you stupid man?" said the old woman.

"I'm telling you: I've brought your daughter back. She was standing out of the rain under the old tree on the road from town."

"My daughter died five years ago under that tree. Now get away from here with your cruel jokes."

The woman slammed the door in the taxi driver's face.

He looked around to ask the girl what this was all about, but she was gone.

STORY TIME

"OK," said Mr. O'Connor, the English teacher, "it's the last lesson of the week. You've worked very well. Let's have a story."

There was a buzz round the class. With a bit of luck, it might be one of Mr. O'Connor's stories about the madman of Manchester who walked on the roof of the station and parachuted off the town hall.

"No," said Mr. O'Connor, "not the madman of Manchester today. I thought we'd have something a bit scary today. Look, it's getting dark. If we switch off the lights, and Ruksana—if you pull those blinds down at the back, David, do the ones at the front, we could make it really spooky."

More buzz. What a great way to end the week. Mr. O'Connor wasn't a bad bloke even if he did shout at you too much. When it was all quiet, he began. It was a long rambling story that, to tell the truth, quite a lot of the class had heard before. Maybe you know it, the one about the man with the golden arm. A rich man dies, a man so rich that when he lost his arm, he had a golden one made in its place. And his son—you probably remember all this—

he got poorer and poorer until one day he had no money, nothing to eat, nothing. So he thinks, "What if I go and dig up my father's grave and get the golden arm." And he does, and he runs home through the street at night with the golden arm under his jacket. But then he starts hearing this little voice behind him: "Give me back my golden arm, give me back my golden arm." So he starts running faster and faster down the road, but the voice follows him: "Give me back my golden arm, give me back my golden arm." Anyway, you probably know it, so I won't go on.

Well, Mr. O'Connor told the whole story and some of the class liked it, some of the class pretended to like it, and some of the class were fed up because they had heard him tell it before. He finished and there was still five minutes left before they went home. The room was dark now and strangely quiet. Then Jason spoke up— Jason, the loner, the one who never played football, the one who stared at the wall all the time and never finished what he was saying.

"It was a good story, sir," says Jason, "but of course it wasn't true. But I know a true story, cos my dad told me."

Everyone listened. From the other side of the room, you could hardly see his face.

"You know my flats, sir, on the other side of the Holloway Road? Well, they're new, aren't they? Where they are now, used to be a factory. It was the Stevens' Ink Factory. You know, where they made ink for pens an' that. My dad used to work there before it got closed down."

Jason's voice was trembling.

23

"They had these great big tubs, you see, where they made the ink. They poured all the different things that made the ink into these tubs and then whopping great big blades sliced it all up and churned it around, right?

"Now then, over the top of these tubs was a place where you could walk. My dad never went along cos he wasn't a foreman or anything. Only the foremen and the inspectors were allowed along. They had to do that to see if all the tubs were working. Well, you know what happened, don't you? One day my dad was working the machines, and the foreman came down the walkway an' he wasn't looking where he was going an' he fell right into one of the tubs. And the blades were going. My dad says they heard this horrible scream that turned into a gurgling noise as he went under. My dad rushed forward to switch off the machine, but it was too late. That foreman bloke was chopped up into mincemeat.

"So now, round by the garages at the back of my flats, if you go out at night, you can sometimes hear this screaming, and then it turns into a gurgling noise and stops. And that's a true story, sir."

The bell went. Mr. O'Connor turned the lights back on. And everyone went home very quietly.

24

MANSOOR AND THE DONKEY

illustrated by Reg Cartwright

Once upon a time there was a man called Mansoor, who lived on the coast of the country we now call Morocco. He was almost alone in the world. All his grandparents were dead. Both his parents were dead. He had no aunts. He had no brothers or sisters. But he did have an old uncle, whom he had never seen. This uncle lived in a village along the valley.

One day Mansoor was sitting in the shade of a tree by a well, when a beautiful young woman came by to fill her waterpot. Mansoor fell in love with her right there and then.

When the woman had filled her waterpot, she began to walk back to the city. Mansoor followed her, not letting her know he was there. He followed her all the way back to the city, through the gate, under the arch, along the narrow streets, through the market, into the shaded high-walled lanes until she came to her home. When he knew where she lived, Mansoor turned and walked back to his own home, on the outskirts of the city.

The next day Mansoor dressed up in his best clothes and went to the woman's home to see her father. He was a merchant, and a very well-off one at that. He took a liking to Mansoor, and Mansoor found out that the beautiful young woman's name was Amina. Mansoor plucked up enough courage to ask Amina's father if he could marry her.

"Of course you can," he said, "but first you must pay me five hundred pieces of silver. That way I will know you are the kind of man who will be able to give Amina a good home, where you can give children a good start in life. If you can manage the five hundred pieces, I promise you, I will pay plenty more than that to set you up in a house together."

Poor Mansoor. He wasn't rich. He had only thirty pieces of silver in the whole world. But he was sure he wanted to marry Amina, so he promised he would bring five hundred pieces of silver to the merchant in ten days' time.

Mansoor left the merchant's house. He

25

walked up and down in the street outside, thinking hard. "Where could he get five hundred pieces of silver? Or where could he get four hundred and seventy pieces of silver to add to the thirty pieces he already had? Crazy! He had no chance of getting four pieces, let alone four hundred and seventy. Why had he said he would find the money? He would look so foolish now. Better not to have said he would try."

Suddenly he stopped. His uncle! The man he had never seen. His only living relative. Surely his uncle would help him. Mansoor had heard people say that he was a very rich man.

Right away he set off down the long, dusty road to his uncle's village. Mansoor walked until the sun went down and the moon rose. He lay down at the side of the road and slept till the sun rose the next morning. He walked again, and as the sun rose in the sky, it got hotter and hotter. The road got dustier and dustier, but Mansoor never stopped for more than a quick drink. And just as the sun was setting again, he arrived in his uncle's village.

He stopped the first person he met and asked the way. It was one of the old men of the village.

"It's down there on the right," he said. "The garden wall is broken, the house is falling down, and you can see the stars through the roof."

"Oh, dear," said Mansoor, "I thought my uncle was a rich man who could help me."

"I don't know about that," said the old man. "He may be rich, but I can tell you this: He doesn't throw his money around."

So Mansoor set off to find his uncle's

tumbledown house. When he got there, he found it was in a terrible state. The garden was like a garbage dump, overgrown with weeds. The walls of the house were cracked and crumbling, and in the cracks, tufts of grass were sprouting and seeding. Not a lick of paint or whitewash had been near the house for years. Even so, Mansoor knew that his uncle was the only chance he had of getting the five hundred pieces of silver.

Outside, he saw an old white donkey tied to a ring on the wall. The donkey was so thin that its bones stuck out and it could hardly stand. The poor thing was starving to death. Mansoor couldn't bear to think of its pain, so he ran straight to the nearest farm and bought a bundle of hay. When he fed it to the donkey, it brayed and pawed the ground as if to say thank you. "Poor thing," thought Mansoor, and he went into the house.

Inside it looked as if nothing had been cleaned, tidied, or put away for twenty years. And the smell! The smell was indescribable. However, his uncle was delighted to see Mansoor, and they sat together and talked about relatives long dead. For supper, all he gave Mansoor was a crust of bread. But Mansoor ate it like it was a good solid meal.

When he had finished, his uncle looked at him and said, "Why have you made the journey to come and see me? In all this time, you've never come before. There must be a reason."

Mansoor went straight to the point.

"I'm hoping that you will lend me five hundred pieces of silver so that I can marry a beautiful woman I have met."

"Oh, no," said the uncle, "oh, dear me, no! I can't lend you anything. I have no money. Can't you see? I'm a very poor old man. Look around you, look at the place. I haven't got any money for myself, let alone to lend to anyone else."

Poor Mansoor. He had walked all that way for nothing. That night he slept on the floor and by the next morning he was bruised all over.

There was nothing to eat, so the uncle said, "Come with me to the market. I'm going to sell that old donkey. It's no use to me now and it eats too much food."

In the marketplace, Mansoor's uncle stood and shouted, "Who'll buy the donkey? Who'll buy the donkey?"

"I'll give you five pieces of silver," said one man. "That's all it's worth. It's a living skeleton."

"I'll give you seven," said another.

"Call it ten," said a third. "You won't do better than that."

Mansoor watched and listened. The donkey was acting strangely. It was looking him straight in the eye and pawing the ground, just as it had done when he had given it the hay the night before.

Mansoor called out to his uncle, "I'll give you twenty pieces for it."

"If that's the way you want it," said the uncle and he took the money, stuffed it into his robe, and with hardly another word, rushed back to his broken-down old house.

Mansoor and the donkey set off on the long walk back to the city. "Now where am I?" he thought. "I set out with thirty pieces of silver to make it up to five hundred, and now all I've got is ten and a rag-and-bone of a donkey. I've only got a few days left to find the money. What can I do?" All the way home, Mansoor's mind was full of such questions.

When Mansoor got home, he had hardly tied up the donkey when there was a knock at the door.

"You are Mansoor?" said the visitor. "I am sorry, but I have bad news. Your uncle has been killed by robbers. They were after the money you gave him for the donkey. They killed him as he was hiding the money. You are his only living relative, and I promised the people of the village I would bring this message. That is all. I must be on my way. Farewell."

And the man galloped away on his horse.

Mansoor was overwhelmed. "I go to my uncle for help, and I end up by bringing him terrible luck. It's my fault he was killed. If I had never gone to see him, he would still be alive today. And it's brought me bad luck too, for now I've got to go all the way back to the village to see to the funeral when I should be here trying to find some way of getting the money. Everything I do goes wrong."

But Mansoor knew that what has to be done has to be done, and he set off once more with the old donkey on the long road back to his uncle's village.

There was a part of him that wanted to think that his uncle *was* a rich man who had gold and silver hidden away, but when he got there the house was empty. There was nothing there. People had taken away the last bits and pieces his uncle had left, and now there was just rubbish. Mansoor scrabbled among it, hoping to find something, but there was nothing.

Now there were only two days left to find the money. He went outside again and sat down on the ground next to the donkey.

"What am I going to do? Ten days ago I had set my heart on marrying the most beautiful woman I have ever seen, and now all I've got is a donkey. I wanted a wife, not a donkey."

But the donkey wasn't listening. It was pawing the ground again.

"Oh, yes, you know what you want, don't you? It's the one thing I seem to know how to do—fetch you hay. Come on, then."

This time Mansoor untied the donkey to let it walk across to the hay itself, but instead it trotted over to the corner of his uncle's yard and started pawing the ground there.

"Oh, you funny old thing," said Mansoor. "That hay over there not good enough for you, eh? Or is it that you want me to feed it to you in your favorite corner?"

So Mansoor, patient as ever, brought the hay over to where the donkey was standing.

No, that wasn't what the beast wanted.

"Water then?" And he fetched water from the well.

But still the donkey pawed the ground.

What a mystery.

"Well, they say donkeys are stupid, and you don't get much more stupid than this. Come on, funny fellow, I can't hang around here much longer. I must get back to the city."

On and on went the donkey with his hoof on the ground.

Suddenly Mansoor realized what was going on. The donkey was telling him that something was there in the ground, where he was scraping his hoof.

"It's me that's stupid, isn't it? You're telling me something, aren't you?"

Mansoor rushed off to get a spade, and he was soon digging away into the ground. At first there was nothing, but Mansoor wouldn't give up. He dug down and down into the ground, deeper and deeper until his spade hit something hollow. He scraped away the earth, and found a wooden chest. He pried open the lid, and there was his uncle's treasure. Hundreds and hundreds of pieces of silver—more than enough to pay Amina's father what he had asked.

Mansoor rushed over to the donkey and flung his arms around the animal's neck.

"Oh, thank you, you clever, clever donkey. I promise you'll have as much hay and water as you want for the rest of your life."

Well, you can guess the rest. Mansoor and the donkey made the journey back to the city once more. He was able to give Amina's father the money. Mansoor and Amina married, set up home, and lived together happily for many, many years—with the old white donkey.

THE STRONGEST PERSON IN THE WORLD

illustrated by Wayne Anderson

Once upon a time there was a family of rats.

When the oldest girl grew up, her mother said, "We must find someone for our oldest daughter to marry."

"Yes," said the father, "she should marry the strongest person in the world, don't you think?"

So Mr. and Mrs. Rat went to see the sun.

"Good morning, Mr. Sun," they said. "We have a fine grown-up daughter and we want to find a husband for her. We want her to marry the strongest person in the world. You sit there right up in the sky, sending out all that heat and light. You seem to be the strongest person in the world. Will you marry our daughter?"

Mr. Sun shook his head and said, "Look, it's very nice of you to think of me like this. Perhaps it seems as if I am the strongest person in the world, but I tell you, I'm not. Not by a long way. You see

Mr. Cloud over there? Now you're talking. He is strong, much stronger than I am. You know, he can cover my face any time he likes and I'm not anywhere near as hot and as light then, am I?"

Mr. and Mrs. Rat thought about that and Mrs. Rat said, "You know, dear, I think Mr. Sun is right. Mr. Cloud must be the strongest person in the world. He's the best one for our daughter."

Next day they went to see Mr. Cloud.

"Good morning, Mr. Cloud. We have a fine grown-up daughter and we're looking for a husband for her. We want her to marry the strongest person in the world. You're so strong, you can cover the face of the sun and stop him from shining, just like that. Please, will you marry our daughter?"

Mr. Cloud smiled and shook his head and said, "Yes, it's true I can cover the sun, but you know it's not me who's the strongest. Think about it, I only cover the

31

sun when the wind blows me. So, you see, Mr. Wind is stronger than I am by far. Believe me, he would make a good husband for your daughter."

Once again, Mr. and Mrs. Rat had a think, and they agreed with Mr. Cloud. Mr. Wind would be the best person for their daughter.

Next day there they were talking to Mr. Wind.

"Good morning, Mr. Wind. We want our daughter to marry the strongest person in the world, and we've worked out, with a little help from some people we've been talking to, that it's you. You're the strongest person in the world. I mean, you can blow away the clouds that cover up the sun any time you want. Please, will you marry our daughter?"

Mr. Wind thought that Mr. and Mrs. Rat were very kind, but that they were wrong.

"No, it's not me who's the strongest. You know who you want? The stone statue of Buddha, the one in Unzin. His feet are so firmly set in the ground that I can't budge him one little bit, no matter how hard I blow. He's got a hat, and you know—I can't even shift that. Now, there's a good husband for your daughter, eh?"

So, after a little chat, off went Mr. and Mrs. Rat to see the stone statue of Buddha in Unzin. Once again they explained what they wanted for their daughter.

"…and at long last we've found who we are sure is the strongest person in the world. So, please marry our daughter."

The stone Buddha spoke to them kindly, "Thank you very much, Mr. and Mrs. Rat, but I'm afraid there is someone who is much stronger than I am. He is the young rat who lives in the ground under my feet. One day, when he is ready, he will dig and dig and dig right under me and you know what will happen to me? I will fall over. And there's nothing in the whole world that I can do about it. Now, how about that rat? Isn't he just the one for your daughter? The wind can shift the cloud to cover up the sun, but it can't shift me. And then along comes that young rat, and he'll be able to do it any time he wants."

Mr. and Mrs. Rat were very happy. They now knew that their oldest girl should marry a young rat, and she would be marrying the strongest person in the whole wide world.

33

DOG, CAT, AND MONKEY

illustrated by Charlotte Voake

Dog and Cat are fighting over some meat. Dog's got his jaws around the bone. Cat's got his claws into the flesh. They heave and they tug, but the moment Dog thinks he's got it, Cat gives it a tug. Then the moment Cat thinks he's got it, Dog gets his teeth around a little more. Neither of them is winning.

Monkey comes to have a look.

Soon he's dancing around, giving advice: "Go on, Cat, go for it with the claws, now the teeth. You've got him now, Dog. Grind those jaws. Don't growl, it'll weaken your grip. Give it a shake, Cat, it'll throw him. Hang on in there, Dog…" and so on.

Dog and Cat start getting tired. Cat has an idea.

While he's hanging on with his claws, he shouts to Monkey, "Say, Monkey, any chance you could help us here? Couldn't you divide it up between us so we each have equal parts?"

Monkey calls back, "I'd love to. We'll just set up some scales to make sure everything's fair, OK?"

So Cat and Dog let go of the meat, and

Monkey starts making some scales with wood and leaves and vines. It's perfect.

"All right," says Monkey, "let's give it a try."

He tears the meat in half and puts half on each side of the scales.

"Ah," says Monkey, "you can see it's not quite an equal half because one side's gone down lower than the other. That means that the meat on that side is just a teeny bit too much. I'll tell you what, I'll just nibble a little off that side to even it up, OK?"

Monkey chews a little off the heavier side and puts the two pieces back on the balance. Cat and Dog are very impressed at his cleverness.

"Oh, whoops!" said Monkey. "I must have chewed a little too much off that side, because look—it's the other side that's lower now. I'll tell you what, I'll just nibble an incy little piece off there, and it'll be ready to divide up."

Monkey chews a piece off the heavier side again and puts the two pieces back on the balance. Cat and Dog lean forward, waiting for the balance to settle. But now the first side goes down again.

"Oh, no," says Monkey. "Well, look at that. I still haven't got it right. But we're nearly there, believe me. You're not long off having your feast, fellers."

Monkey chews a little more off the meat and puts the two pieces back.

"Here we go," says Monkey, "this is it."

Once again Cat and Dog get ready to eat, but yet again one side goes down lower.

"Oh, dear, oh, dear, oh, dear," says Monkey. "This isn't going quite as I planned. But we must get it right, or you two will be arguing about this for years and years, eh?"

Monkey takes another bite off the meat and to tell the truth, there isn't much left. Now, when he puts the two pieces on the balance, one is mostly bone and the other is just a sliver of meat. Monkey is most upset.

"This isn't going right at all, is it?"

At that, he stuffs the last piece of meat into his mouth, tosses the bone away, and leaps up into the tree.

There he wipes his mouth and calls down to Dog and Cat, "Say fellers, any time you've got something to divide up, just bring it along to me, and I'll be glad to help you again."

HARE, HIPPO, AND ELEPHANT

illustrated by Christopher Brown

Hare was a lazy thing, and when he got married and settled down he couldn't be bothered to get down to hard work. Go out and work in the fields so he could feed his wife and himself? Not on your life.

Then one day he had an idea.

He took a long rope and went into the forest to find Hippo.

"Hippo, will you listen to me a moment? Why don't we have a game here. I tie this rope to you, and I'll see if I can pull you out of the mud."

"Right," said Hippo, "sounds like a great game to me, one I can't lose."

"Good," said Hare, "so I'll go off among the trees over there. The moment you feel a tug on the rope, you pull like mad, OK? But I'm warning you, I'm pretty strong."

Hippo laughed. "Yes, of course you are, Hare."

Hare tied the rope around Hippo and then went off among the trees and waited. It wasn't long before Elephant came down to the water hole.

Hare stopped him. "Oh, Elephant, have you got a moment? I'm looking for someone who wants a tug-of-war. Everyone I challenge, I beat. What do you say?"

"Out of my way, little fool. I haven't got time to play silly games."

"No, listen, Elephant, I tell you what, if you win, I'll do anything you want. I'll be your servant, I'll fetch and carry, anything."

Elephant liked the sound of that very much indeed. So he let Hare tie the rope around him and off went Hare, telling Elephant to start pulling when he felt a tug on the rope.

Halfway along the rope, where neither Hippo nor Elephant could see him, Hare gave a tug on the rope, first one way and then the other. At once, Elephant and Hippo started heaving on the rope. They heaved and they pulled for hours. The sun went down, and they heaved all night. The sun came up again, and still they heaved until they could heave no more and fell down exhausted.

They rested, and when they staggered to their feet both animals wondered just how Hare had managed it and started walking toward each other. When they met, they untied the rope from each other's waists.

"Next time we see Hare, let's kill him," they said.

The next day Hare went out and was rather pleased to see that the ground was all churned up. "Just ready to plant my seeds in," he thought, "and just think, I didn't even have to do any heavy digging and ploughing. Won't my wife be pleased with me!"

38

WHY DO DOGS CHASE CARS?

illustrated by Michael Foreman

Everyone in West Africa knows why dogs chase cars.

Some time ago, when cars first came to the roads, a donkey, a goat, and a dog took a ride in a taxi. They were off out of town, to the villages where they lived.

When they reached the first village, the donkey tapped the driver on the shoulder. "This is where I'm getting out, driver," he said. "How much?"

"Three thousand francs," said the driver.

The donkey paid up and on went the goat and the dog in the taxi.

Soon the goat asked to be dropped off.

"How much?" he asked.

"Three thousand francs," said the driver.

The goat didn't hang around. He jumped from the taxi and scampered off into the bush.

At long last, the dog got to where he wanted to go.

"How much?" said the dog.

"Three thousand francs," said the driver.

Dog held up a five-thousand-franc note. The driver grabbed the note and drove off down the road roaring with laughter.

So now you know why a donkey, a goat, and a dog all do different things when a car comes down the road.

Donkeys just stay right where they are. They let the driver go around them. They know they paid up. They've done nothing wrong, so they've got nothing to be ashamed of.

The moment a car comes down the road and there's a goat around, it'll scamper off as fast it can because it knows that it didn't pay the fare and the driver is looking for his money.

But dogs spend their whole time chasing cars, looking for the driver who once cheated them.

THE BEGINNING OF HISTORY

illustrated by Cathie Felstead

Before the beginning of time, before the beginning of everything, before there was a beginning, there was Ngutapa. He had no father. He had no mother.

Ngutapa had a wife called Mapana who had grown up with him.

It was at this time that the earth was beginning to take shape. The forests were no more than little plants in the ground, and the great rivers were no more than little trickles of water.

Many years went by. Ngutapa and Mapana never lived together, never had any children. One day they were out hunting, and Ngutapa shot a dart at an animal but missed. Mapana cursed him for missing, but Ngutapa blamed Mapana for frightening the animal before he shot the dart. This was the start of a terrible quarrel. In the end Ngutapa grabbed Mapana and tied her to a tree. He left her there and went off hunting on his own.

Little by little, one at a time to begin with, the ants and the wasps came and bit Mapana. Soon they came in their tens and then in their hundreds.

Ayeeee, she suffered, how she suffered. But then the Canca bird appeared and sat at the top of the tree that she was tied to.

Mapana called out to it, "Can you untie me? Please can you untie me?"

"*Co, co, co, coo*," called the bird.

"Listen, Canca, that fool Ngutapa has tied me up so that the wasps and ants will sting me to death. Please untie me."

And now the Canca bird turned into a man and came close to Mapana.

"What happened to you, my child? I will untie you. But listen, if you want to get your own back on Ngutapa, I have a wasps' nest here. Keep it and you will make him squeal with pain."

The man untied Mapana, and she took the wasps' nest.

"But you can't stay here," said the man. "You must wait somewhere where Ngutapa can't see you."

At that, the man turned back into the Canca bird and flew off.

After a while, Ngutapa came back from hunting. When he saw that Mapana wasn't there, he was so pleased. He took out his flute and played and sang:

"Oh, where can Mapana be?
The wasps and ants have bitten her.
Oh, where can Mapana be?
The wasps and ants have eaten her.
Cherroo-roo, cherroo-roo,
Cherroo-roo-rooooooo."

But Mapana was hiding in the hollow of

a tree, just waiting for Ngutapa to walk by. She heard his singing and got herself ready, and then, just as he came dancing past, she hurled the wasps' nest at him and hit him on the legs. Out flew the wasps and stung and stung and stung him. Mostly they stung his knees and in no time at all they swelled up so badly that Ngutapa could hardly drag himself home.

Once he got there, he climbed into his hammock. Mapana saw him come back, but she said nothing. She didn't speak to him, she didn't look at him, she didn't move toward him. She would have nothing at all to do with him.

Night fell, and his knees were hurting more and more. Now he cried pitifully. *Ayeeee*, how he suffered. As the days passed, his knees got bigger and bigger. And now, as the skin stretched, it became as clear as a mountain stream. You could see straight through the skin and right into his knees.

Ngutapa looked in and saw two people. He looked across to his other knee, and there were two more. The following day he could see in one of his knees a boy making a blowpipe and a girl weaving a basket. Again he looked across to the other knee, and it was the same.

Another day went by and with a sudden rush, his knees split open. Ngutapa looked down, and out from his knees came men with their blowpipes and women with their baskets.

After that, Ngutapa was all right. The pain passed, and there were people on earth to hunt and fish and start the human race.

SUNKAISSA, THE GOLDEN-HAIRED PRINCESS

illustrated by Graham Percy

Once long ago, in the mountains, a huge and horrible monster fell in love with a golden-haired princess called Sunkaissa. He watched her going about her work, and one day, when she was out working, he seized her and took her off to his cave higher up the mountain.

Sunkaissa's family was overcome with despair and sadness that they had lost their beautiful girl.

But her oldest brother was a brave young man and he said, "Listen, we'll never get her back sitting around here crying. I'm going to go up the mountain and find her."

"No," said his father, "the monster has taken her. You're no match for him. He'll tear you apart with one blow. Isn't it

bad enough that we've lost a daughter? We don't want to lose a son as well."

But the young man wouldn't listen.

"I can't sit here, knowing that the monster has her in his clutches. I'd rather die than put up with it."

Off he went, up, up the mountain, but there was no sign of his sister. He crossed right over the top down onto the other side. He crossed valleys, rivers, forests, but never a sign of the monster or Sunkaissa. Then one day he was sitting by a stream when he glanced down and saw, there in the grass, some long golden hairs. "Surely these must belong to Sunkaissa," he thought. "If I follow the stream, I'll find her."

46

Off he went, following the stream, looking out for signs. Then, glancing up from the ground, he caught sight of a great dark cave in the rocks. He hid behind a tree and watched and waited. It wasn't long before a young woman with long golden hair came out. She sat down on the grass and started combing her hair. It was Sunkaissa. Her brother crept closer to her, not wanting to surprise her and make her call out. Just as he was close by, she dropped her comb.

And as she did this, she said, without so much as a glance up at the person who had made a shadow on the ground beside her, "Please pick up my comb for me."

The brother picked up her comb and handed it to her, but he could see that Sunkaissa didn't know him or recognize him. So he sang to her a song with a tune that they had sung together when they were young:

"I am your brother, one of your own,
I've traveled the mountains to find you.
I've looked in the fields, I've looked by
*   the streams,*
And now I've found you. You can
*   come home."*

It could have been the words, it could have been the tune—Sunkaissa now recognized her brother. And she was frightened.

"I can't come, dear brother. The monster will catch us and tear us to bits."

"Well, hide me somewhere near so that I can have time to think how we can get rid of the monster."

"You can hide in the cow shed," said Sunkaissa. "In there is a cow. Nothing like one you've ever seen before. Enormous. Gigantic. When she moos, jump into her mouth and hide. Go now, quickly, before the monster comes back."

The brother dashed off to the cow shed, and there was the biggest cow the world has ever seen. He climbed up onto a beam and when the cow mooed, he jumped into its mouth. There he sat till the evening.

Suddenly, there came a great shaking of the ground and a great roaring in the air. The door of the cow shed crashed open, and there stood the monster.

"I smell the smell of a human being," he roared.

"No," said the cow. "You've got it wrong. There's no human being in here."

"Don't lie to me, cow," said the monster. "When I say there's a human being in here, then there's a human being."

"Well, now," said the cow, "I'll tell you what. I've always wanted to know how many hairs there are on my body. If you could count all the hairs on my body, then I might be able to find a human being for you."

"Very well," growled the monster, and he started counting. This shouldn't take me long, he thought.

"1, 2, 3…234…8976…one million…

(the hours were passing and the monster's eyes were beginning to get tired, but on he went)…two million…three million, three million and one…"

Just then the cow shivered—a great big shaky shiver—and the monster lost his place.

"I don't know where I was!" he shouted.

"Oh, really?" said the cow. "I'm so sorry. Don't worry, start again and I'm sure you'll get it right next time."

The monster started again, and this time he got to four million and nineteen when the cow gave another great shaky shiver and the monster lost his place again. Well, this went on for hours and hours. Every time the monster got anywhere near counting all the hairs, the cow shivered. Little by little, the monster began to get tired. His head drooped and he started to mutter.

"Three milly, four humble, bendy boo tousled, two humble and bendy tree; three milly, four humble, bendy boo tousled, two humble and bendy floor; three milly, four humble, bendy boo—" and he flopped to the floor fast asleep.

Out of the cow's mouth jumped the brother, who leapt onto the monster and killed him. He ran to find Sunkaissa, and together they made the long journey home. You can imagine how overjoyed their family and the people of the village were to see them, and how they loved hearing the story of the cow.

And you know, if you watch a cow, you can see to this day that, whether she's in the field or the cow shed, every ten minutes or so she gives a shaky shiver.

EARS, EYES, LEGS, AND ARMS

illustrated by Louise Brierley

Once, long ago, the different parts of the body weren't all together but went around the world on their own. The ears, the eyes, the legs, and the arms all went about their business, doing what they had to do—ears one way, eyes the other, legs off over there, arms over the other way.

One day though, they decided to go out hunting together. The ears, eyes, legs, and arms marched off to the forest.

They walked for seven days before they got there, but just as they were getting near, the ears called out, "Shh, listen! I can hear something."

Immediately the eyes started to search among the trees, and then suddenly they called out, "There! Look! An antelope! Over there…"

The legs set off to chase it, followed closely by the arms.

As the legs caught up with the antelope, the arms reached out and killed it.

After a while, the ears and the eyes caught up with their friends.

"What do you want?" said the arms. "The antelope's ours. We caught it. Go away."

"No, come off it," said the legs. "You would never have been able to grab it if it wasn't for us being fast enough to catch up with it."

"Never mind that," said the eyes. "I reckon the antelope's ours, because we were the ones who saw it. You wouldn't have known where to go if it wasn't for us."

"All right, all right," said the ears. "Who got the whole thing going? Us, of course. We heard the antelope, didn't we? You'd all be sitting around back there if it

50

51

wasn't for us hearing it move."

Just then a mosquito came by.

"What's going on? What's all the fuss about?"

They told it the story.

"Hmm," said the mosquito, "this is a tricky one. Very tricky. But listen, there's a wise old chief not far from here—why not take the problem to him?"

Off went the four friends to the wise old chief, with the arms carrying the antelope.

The chief listened to the story and then ordered the antelope to be cooked. When it was brought to him, he sat down and started eating. He didn't stop until he had finished every last bit. And not once did he ask the four friends to have some.

Then the chief spoke. "I listened to your story and decided that I would punish all of you for being so mean and selfish. First I punished you by eating all of the antelope without sharing any of it with you. Now I am going to punish you all once more by joining you together so that something like this never happens again."

And he did.

The parts of the body were furious with the chief for doing this, but they were even angrier with the mosquito for bringing them to see the chief. And that's why whenever the ears hear the whine of a mosquito, the eyes search for it, and the arms try and slap it. If, as often happens, the mosquito still whines even after the arms have slapped and smacked all over the place, the legs join in the hunt.

52

THE LION AND THE HARE

illustrated by James Marsh

Once upon a time many years ago, Tau the lion met Mmutla the hare.

Mmutla thought to himself, as he saw Tau coming toward him, "Here comes the king of the beasts. I will try to trick him."

So Mmutla said to the lion, "Good morning, Your Majesty. You must be very lonely and sad, living on your own. May I come and live with you?"

Tau the lion grunted and looked hard at the hare, but he didn't say anything.

So Mmutla the hare continued, "Surely you don't like doing all your own cooking, cleaning, and washing? Let me come and do all your work. Let me come and cook for you. Let me come and clean for you. Let me come and wash for you. I could do all your hard work. You are much too important to do everything for yourself."

The lion thought for a moment, then he said, "It would be nice to have someone else to do all my cooking and cleaning and washing. And people say that hares are good at housework. Mmmm, it's very tempting…I tell you what, I will find the food, you can cook it and wash up afterward. You can keep my home tidy and do all the hard work. Good, I like it. And don't try and trick me, understand?"

"Would I?" said the hare. "Would I try and trick you? Perish the thought. You've made a good bargain—you fetch the food, I cook it. And believe me, I'm not afraid of hard work."

So Tau the lion showed the hare where he had his home.

Mmutla the hare pretended to be shocked.

"But this won't do for the king of the beasts. It's much too uncomfortable. We must build a fine comfortable house."

"Very good idea," said the lion. "I've certainly got a servant with the right ideas here," he thought. "Let's start at once."

The lion and the hare started work on the new house right away. They worked nonstop for days. Hare fetched and carried and lifted hour after hour. Tau the lion just could not believe his luck. Here was a real servant.

They were nearly finished when Mmutla the hare said, "Look, I'm really hungry. Why don't we sit down and have something to eat?"

"No!" said the lion. "I decide what happens around here. I am the master and you are the servant. We'll eat when we've finished. The last job to do is putting the roof on. When that's done, we'll eat. Now, no more moaning, and get on with it or you'll have nothing at all."

So they set to work putting the roof on. Tau the lion held the grass in place, and Mmutla the hare threaded the great needle in and out of the grass, tying it to the beams. Then, as quick as lightning, the hare slipped a loop of the thread over the lion's front paw. Then, just as quickly again, he slipped a loop over the lion's other front paw. Tau was tied to the roof of the hut. He couldn't move. He struggled, he roared. He roared, he struggled, but it was no use.

Mmutla the hare just laughed.

"Now, what was it you were saying about my not having my dinner till we had finished? Well, I tell you what—I'll have my dinner now. I'm so sorry you can't join me."

So while the lion struggled and wriggled, Mmutla the hare finished all the food.

But lions are very strong, and it wasn't long before the thread broke and Tau was free. He jumped down and chased the hare. You can be sure Mmutla was scared, really scared. He ran like he had never run before. He ran till he saw a hole in the ground and bolted down it—just in time.

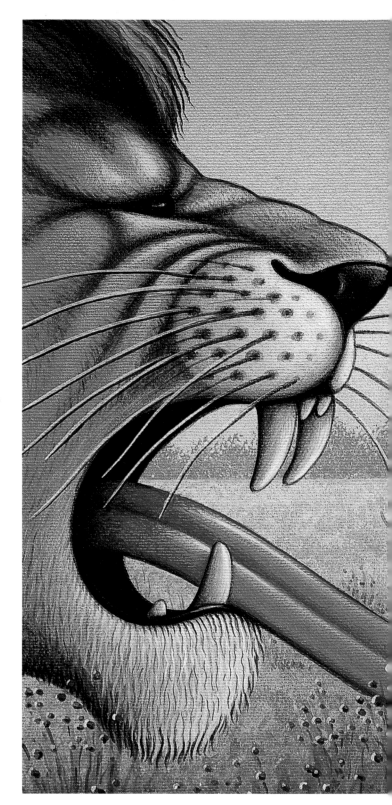

54

But Tau thrust his great paw down the hole and grabbed hold of Mmutla's leg. Mmutla tried digging his claws into the ground, but slowly Tau the lion was dragging him out of the hole. "What am I going to do?" thought the hare.

Then he shouted out as loud as he could, "You'll never get me out. That's not my leg you've got hold of there. It's the root of the tree. You might pull the tree down, but you won't get me, you big mutt."

Tau let go of Mmutla's leg and made a grab for anything else he could feel. This time it *was* the root of the tree.

"Ah," shouted Mmutla, "right, you've got my leg now. I should never have told you that."

So Tau heaved and pulled on the root while the hare hurried on down deep into the hole. The hole ran along for a good way and then came up about fifty feet from where Tau the lion was still tugging on the tree root.

Up popped Mmutla the hare. "Cooee, you old fool. Thanks for letting me go. What a friend you are."

And off he ran, with the lion pounding along behind him.

It wasn't long before Tau caught up with the hare, right on the banks of a deep river. "I must get across here, whatever else happens," thought Mmutla.

Tau pounced on him and held him in his great paws.

"Oh, mighty one," sobbed Mmutla. "Oh, you don't know how sorry I am. I am truly sorry for what I have done. It was a mean trick and it will never happen again.

Look, you can do anything that you want with me. Kill me, eat me, feed me to the birds, but whatever you do, keep me away from my worst enemy. He lives on the other side of the river. Over there. Please, I beg of you, don't let him get his hands on me or I'll die the most agonizing death the world has ever seen."

Tau the lion laughed, "Ah ha-hah! I'll make you sorry, all right. I'll make you sorry that you tried to trick the king of the beasts. I don't think I can come up with a horrible enough way for you to die, but your enemy over there seems to have the right idea. I *will* give you to him, no matter what you say."

At that, Tau the lion flung Mmutla as hard as he could over the river.

When he landed on the other side, Mmutla called back to the lion, "Thanks. You're a real friend. I haven't got any enemies over here, you dumb dolt. All you've just done is help me get away from *you*."

And off he ran.

Now Tau was angry. Actually he wasn't just angry, he was furious. He could have roared the forest down if he had tried. He caught sight of a log floating down the river and he leapt onto it. Meanwhile, Mmutla was running along thinking he was safe, but the log was floating faster and faster down the river, after Mmutla. It wasn't long before the log got close enough to the riverbank for the lion to leap from it and onto the bank. And now he hurtled after the hare.

Mmutla had slowed down to a jog and was looking around himself, thinking how clever he had been. Tau the lion caught sight of him, slowed down, crouched, and inched nearer and nearer. Then with one great bound, he leapt out of the bushes right onto the hare. Mmutla was well and truly caught.

"Now I'm done for," thought Mmutla. "This is the end."

But even as he was thinking this, he was looking around him, trying to find some way out.

"Now you've caught me once and for all, oh great one. These are my last moments on earth. And I deserve to be eaten. I only say this: Don't forget to say your prayers, and thank God for what you are about to eat."

"Quite right," thought Tau, "I should thank God." And he closed his eyes to pray. The moment he did, Mmutla the hare grabbed a stone and hurled it into a bees' nest he had noticed in the tree above them. The bees went crazy and swarmed around looking for who had disturbed them.

Mmutla made off like the wind, but Tau the lion sat there with his eyes shut, thanking God with all his might. Down came the bees straight toward him. They stung every bit of him they could find, and when they couldn't find any more bits to sting, they stung the stung bits all over again. It was weeks before he was well enough to think about chasing Mmutla again.

But now he had the memory of all that pain to spur him on.

"I'll catch that revolting little hare if it's the last thing I ever do. I don't mind how long I have to wait, but I'll get him."

His chance came not long after. He caught sight of Mmutla asleep by some rocks. He crept nearer and nearer...and jumped. But Mmutla wasn't asleep. He was just resting with one eye open on the lookout for danger. Just when Tau was in midair, flying toward him, Mmutla the hare leapt out from under the lion. The lion landed on the ground with a thud, but Mmutla didn't run off. He leapt at the rocks.

"Quick! Quick!" he shouted. "I've just saved your life. Didn't you see it? When you jumped just then, you disturbed the rocks. If I hadn't leapt up here to hold that one back, you'd have been crushed to death by it."

"Wow," said Tau the lion. "Thanks, thanks a lot."

"Don't just stand there thanking me," said the hare. "Come over here and help me. You're much stronger than I am. Get your shoulder behind this and you'll be safe."

Up jumped Tau, and he wedged his body under the rock and heaved.

"Whatever you do now," said Mmutla the hare, "don't let go or you'll be crushed to death. You're doing a great job there. Stick with it. I'll rush off and get some help." At that, Mmutla patted the lion on the head and off he ran as fast as he could.

Tau strained and heaved against that rock for days before he realized that he had been tricked. And when he did, he felt very, very silly. Mmutla, by now, was a long, long way away, and Tau never saw him again.

THE
FOUR BROTHERS

illustrated by Christopher Corr

Ram Lal was a rich farmer. He had a huge farm. He also had four sons: Roop, Veer, Yash, and Dheer. Ram Lal loved his sons and wanted to do all he could for them. But even though he wasn't very old, one day he became very ill and was afraid that he was going to die.

He called his sons to his bedside and said, "Listen, boys, I'm very rich and I don't think I've got long to live in this world. If I die, please remember what I am saying to you now. This big farm and the house belong to you all. Live together, love each other, and work hard. Try to be

cheerful in what you do; stay happy. Some time from now, you may think you want to divide the farm among you and live apart from each other. If this happens, then the first thing you must do is go and talk to my brother, Sham Lal. Listen to what he says."

Not long after, Ram Lal died and the four brothers started their life together. The oldest two, Roop and Veer, liked looking after the farm. They worked hard, raised good crops, and soon the brothers were getting richer and richer. The younger brothers, Yash and Dheer, spent

58

their time reading and writing and thinking, studying all the books they could get hold of.

Years passed and the four brothers each got married. They and their wives all still lived together and they were very happy.

But then arguments started. The wives of the two oldest brothers weren't sure that things were fair on the farm.

One day Roop's wife said to Veer's wife, "Have you noticed? Your husband and mine do all the work around here, while the other two spend their time lolling around reading and writing. Our husbands make the money; the other two spend it. It's not fair, is it?"

After this first conversation, they could hardly stop thinking and talking about it. In the end, they went to their husbands. But when Roop's wife spoke to Roop about it, he was furious.

"Don't you ever, ever say my brothers are lazy. Never say things like that."

But she did. She would talk about it whenever she could. And Veer's wife did the same.

One day the older brothers and their wives met up for a talk. They arranged to meet up with the younger brothers and their wives. This happened, and they all agreed that the time had come to split up the farm and divide it among them.

"One thing, though," said one brother. "We did promise Father that we would talk to his brother, Sham Lal, first."

When they went to see Sham Lal, he had some words for them. "I tell you what, before you divide the farm among you, why don't you each go off for a while?

Leave home and try and earn a little money. Then come back again."

Next morning off went the four brothers, each going a different way.

Roop didn't go far. In the next village, a farmer needed some help with ploughing and sowing. His bullocks were frisky and wouldn't pull the plough. Roop took hold of them and soon got them working. The farmer was very pleased with him and paid him one rupee for his work. Well, Roop was very pleased that he had earned all that money so quickly, and he went home with it right away.

Veer went to a village a little farther off. He found that the villagers were in trouble. Their land had dried up, and nothing was growing because the local river had changed direction. It wasn't watering their land anymore. Veer called the villagers together and took them upstream and showed them how to make a dam across the river. The villagers worked at it. They built the dam, and then made a canal that ran from the dam into their fields so their crops could grow again.

The villagers were very pleased with Veer. They paid him one hundred rupees for all his help, and Veer came home with the money.

Yash, the third brother, traveled to a nearby town.

In the marketplace, he asked, "Who are the really important people around here?" and he was sent off to see a rich merchant.

"Pleased to be of service to you," said Yash.

"Ah, you've come at a bad time for us," said the merchant, "but perhaps you can help. I am one of four brothers. Our father died not long ago. We divided up his house and land. That all went fine, but there was a family cat. All of us wanted it, but we couldn't divide it up between us. So what we decided on, and I think you'll agree this is a good idea, we decided we should all own the cat but each one of us should own one of its legs.

"Now one day the cat had an accident, and the leg belonging to me got hurt. I put a bandage on the leg and let the cat go. It was winter. The cat went and sat near the fire, and the loose end of the bandage caught fire. The cat was so frightened that it ran around the house setting fire to the whole building. The house was completely destroyed. All my brothers said that the house was burnt down by the fire from the bandage on the leg that belonged to me. So now they say that I've got to build them a new house or pay them for it.

"They say that they'll take me to court if I don't, and I'll have to go to prison. But you see, I don't think it's my fault that the house caught fire. I don't see why I should pay them for it."

Yash said he would help the merchant settle the matter.

He called all the brothers together and said, "You have all lost a lot because your house was burnt down. Of course, whoever is to blame must pay or rebuild the house. Now, it is true that it was the bandage on one of the cat's legs that set fire to the house. It is also true that this was the leg that belonged to my friend and your brother the merchant, and so you three are asking him to pay up. But think of this. If the cat had had only one leg, it couldn't have run around. It could only run around and set fire to the building because it had the other three legs. So it was the other three legs that are to blame. It's their fault that the house got burnt down, and let me remind you, those three legs belong to you other three brothers. If you really want to say that some of you are more to blame than others, then it's you who should be paying for the new house and not the merchant."

The other three thought that Yash had said some good things there, and so all four brothers agreed that they'd each give a quarter of the cost of rebuilding their house. Of course, the merchant was very pleased that Yash had saved him all that money and he paid him a thousand rupees.

"It would be a good idea if you stayed in the city and helped other people the way you've helped me," said the merchant.

"Indeed, I would like to," said Yash, "but first I must go home and see my brothers."

Dheer, the youngest brother, went to the main city of the area. There he heard that the king's chief minister was soon going to lose his job because he couldn't do what the king had asked him. Dheer went to see the chief minister to find out just what it was that the king was asking him to do.

But the chief minister was very worried and wouldn't say anything to Dheer.

"No one can help me. It's no use my saying. No one."

But Dheer pleaded with him.

"Just tell me. I may well be able to help you. All you need to do is tell me and then we'll see."

At last the minister said, "Our king has a huge elephant. He has asked me to find out how much the elephant weighs. But how can you find out how much an elephant weighs? You can't put it on a pair of scales. You know, I think the king just wants to get rid of me and that is why he is asking me to solve this problem. He has ordered me to find out in seven days, and if I don't I'll lose my job. You know what day it is now? The sixth day. Tomorrow I'm finished. Finished."

Dheer listened carefully and then said, "Sir, don't worry. Tomorrow I will weigh the elephant. Bring it to the river in the morning. Bring a large boat too, and a pair of scales."

The next morning, the minister brought the elephant to the river with the boat and the scales. Dheer got the elephant to step into the boat. The boat sank down into the water, and Dheer stepped up and marked the side of the boat just at the point where the water now reached. Then he led the elephant back off the boat again and with the help of some

61

people, filled the boat with sand.

The boat began to sink down into the water. Just at the moment when it reached the mark he had made on the side, he called out, "Stop!"

Then he took the pair of scales and bucket by bucket he weighed out all the sand in the boat. When he had finished, he knew exactly how much the elephant weighed.

The minister was over the moon, he was so pleased. He ran off to the king to tell him.

"Who helped you find this out?" said the king. "Bring him here."

Dheer was brought before the king.

"You're a clever young man," said the king. "You've done very well. I would like you to be one of my ministers and help me here."

"Indeed, I would most like to, Your Majesty," said Dheer, "but first I must go home and talk to my brothers."

The minister paid Dheer two thousand rupees for the work he had done and Dheer went home.

The four brothers and their wives met their uncle, Sham Lal. Each of the brothers told his story. When they had finished, Sham Lal said, "Now, if you want to, you can divide up the farm between you."

But the four brothers and their wives said, "No, we don't want to divide things up. We'll stay together as long as we live."

Yash and Dheer had to go because they had promised to return to the merchant and to the king. They left their share of the farm for their brothers to look after, and each year sent money home to them.

THE WILD PIGS

illustrated by Helen Oxenbury

In the summer, little Georgiou always took his mother's goats to the forest. He stayed there all day and didn't go home till it was dark. One night, when he got home, Georgiou found his mother sitting on the floor crying.

"A dreadful thing has happened. The wild pigs are eating our grapes, and we won't have any to sell. What are we going to do? I work too hard all day. I can't sit up at night frightening away the pigs. We are ruined."

Georgiou grabbed the wooden spoon and banged it down on the table.

"I am the man of the house," he said. "I will sit up at night and drive the pigs away. I'll make a big noise with the spoon on the copper pot and sleep in the daytime when I'm looking after the goats."

"But you're only a little boy," said his mother, "and the wild pigs may not be afraid of you. Some of those pigs are as big as donkeys."

"Even donkeys can get scared," said Georgiou. "I will try."

After the meal, he went out with the spoon and the pot and climbed up a fig tree in the vineyard. The moon was out, and Georgiou stared out over the vines. It wasn't long before the pigs arrived. A huge mother pig, the size of a donkey, snuffled her way into the vineyard with a litter of little pigs behind her. Soon they were on to the grapes, snuffling and grunting, tearing down the vines, trampling all over the tender young plants.

Georgiou gathered the spoon and the pot together and banged for all his worth, but

64

it didn't make a bit of difference. On they went, snuffling and grunting and guzzling at the grapes.

So now Georgiou slipped down the tree and waited at the edge of the field. It wasn't long before one of the little pigs, straying from its mother, came grunting and snuffling along right up to where he was standing. He waited for his moment and then with a quick lunge, he leapt forward, grabbed its two back legs, and ran to the fig tree and climbed back up.

The little pig squealed like a crazy thing, but Georgiou wouldn't let go. Now the mother pig came hunting for her piglet and charged at the bottom of the tree. That fig tree shook and shook, but Georgiou wouldn't come down, and it was keeping her away from the grapes. It wasn't long before some men from the village came because they had heard the beating on the copper pot and wondered what it was. They drove the pigs out of the field and promised that they would build the fence up around the vineyard in the morning, so that no more pigs would come in and steal the grapes.

As for Georgiou, he had a little wild pig for a pet. A mother dog fed her with her own milk and she lived till she grew up.

SNAKE, HORSE, AND TOAD

illustrated by Clare Melinsky

Once upon a time there was a snake who owned a fine horse. The snake was very proud of his horse. He liked to go riding, to show it off to all the other animals. One day he took the horse out for a ride and as usual, he sat coiled up in the saddle, feeling so proud and fine sitting there.

It wasn't very long before he came across a toad.

"Hey," shouted Toad, "look at you. Don't you know the right way to ride a horse? Get down from there and I'll show you."

Snake was worried. Maybe he wasn't putting on quite such a show as he had hoped. So he slithered down from the horse. Up hopped Toad.

"Watch this, Snake," said Toad. "See how I look straight ahead of me—my back's very straight, and my knees are bent. Watch how I hold the reins as I put the horse through its paces. Dress right, dress left, then walk, trot, canter, gallop, turn, and halt."

It was an amazing show. Not once did Toad stumble or swerve.

"There now, Snake. That's riding. I don't know what you call what you've been doing."

Down hopped Toad and up went Snake again. But once again, he coiled himself up in the saddle, and the horse ambled along in the same old sloppy, jerky way.

Toad was furious.

"That's not what I showed you, you clumsy oaf!" he shouted. "Look at you. You're slouching, you're swaying all over the place, and the horse doesn't know whether it's coming or going. Ride like I do, or you might as well not bother to ride at all."

But Snake didn't even look back. He didn't show even the smallest sign that he had heard what Toad was saying.

In fact, he was muttering very quietly, "What you say is probably right. Thing is, I own a horse and you don't."

And he rode on down the road and out of sight while the toad sat there, still fuming.

GOOD MORNING

illustrated by Janet Woolley

There were once two men passing each other on the road.

"Hey," says one, "why didn't you say good morning?"

"Why didn't *you* say good morning?"

"Well, why should I be the first one to say it?" says the first.

"Well, why should I, for that matter?" says the second.

They argued this way and that for quite some time, until one of them said, "I'll tell you what, whoever can do something for a prince wins this silly argument, and the other one will have to say good morning."

So the first man says, "I'll try first," and he made his way to the palace. After some time, he managed to get an audience with the prince.

"What can I do for you, Your Majesty?" said the man.

And the prince said, "On the other side of the river lives a princess. No one can ever get to see her, visit her, or talk to her. Will you go there and ask her if she will marry me?"

So off went the man. He crossed the river by boat and came to the princess's palace gate.

"Stop! Who goes there?" shouted the guards.

"I have a message for the princess," said the man.

At once, the guards said, "The princess does not like men. She will see no one."

"But listen, I don't come for my sake. I don't come for some ordinary man. I come from a prince, the prince from the other side of the river."

The guards weren't sure about it but let him through all the same.

Inside the palace, he was able to meet the princess.

Immediately he bowed down before her. "Your Majesty, I come from the prince on the other side of the river. He sends his greetings and best regards to you and asks you for your hand in marriage."

The princess stared at the man and then turned away saying, "I will marry no one. Men! I hate them and despise them. Contemptible creatures."

She got up to go.

"But, Your Majesty," said the man, "before you go, could I perhaps take some message to the prince?"

"No," said the princess, still leaving.

"But—but then could I give him some idea of why it is that you hate men?"

"Yes, I will tell you. Once in another life, I was a bird. I had a husband, and he promised me that he would stay with me at all times. He promised me that he would stay with me through flood or fire, through cold or heat. One day when I was sitting on my eggs, a stupid man came to the forest and lit a fire. It started to set the whole forest ablaze. I stayed with my eggs and burned to death. I came back as a human. But what of my husband? The moment he smelled smoke, he was away faster than the tiger on the forest floor. He deserted me. Men! I hate them."

At that, she turned away and strode out of the room. The man went back to the prince and told him everything. The next day, the prince went to visit the princess across the river. When he finally got to see her, he fell to his knees.

"Madam, please hear me. Once in another life, I was a bird and I had a lovely wife. We lived together in the forest. One day a stupid, stupid man came and lit a fire. It set the whole forest alight, but in this life I am a prince and I would dearly love to marry you."

The princess listened and then slowly and sadly said, "I was your wife."

"You were my wife?" said the prince. "But I thought you had flown away. I couldn't see you in the smoke."

And the princess said again, "I am your wife. I thought you had flown away and deserted me."

"Oh, no," said the prince, "I would never have done that. I was looking for you."

The princess breathed in deeply. "Will you marry me?" she said.

"That's all I want in the whole world," said the prince.

Well, they got married, which meant that the man had done something for a prince. So off he goes to find the other man.

"I did something for a prince," he says.

"Good morning," says the other.

PEDRO AND HIS DOG

illustrated by John Burningham

igh up in the Andes mountains, where it is cold and the people wear warm woollen capes called ponchos, was a farm belonging to a little boy called Pedro and his family. They lived in the city, but once a year Pedro and his father visited the farm. For the rest of the year, the farm and the animals were cared for by the farm workers.

This year as Pedro and his father arrived at the farm on their horses, a pack of skinny dogs came running up, barking, howling, and snapping with their fierce sharp teeth. The farm workers called the dogs off, and they ran away snarling and growling. Just one dog was friendly and tame. He came up wagging his tail, letting Pedro stroke him.

It was very cold on the farm, and the farm workers gave Pedro and his father warm ponchos to wear. So now when Pedro or his father went climbing over the mountains, the dogs didn't come snapping after them because they thought they were farm workers too.

Pedro made the friendly dog his pet, and it followed him everywhere. He made a kennel for it and gave it little bits and pieces from his dinner.

One day one of the farm workers came up to him. "You're too kind to that dog. You stroke him and feed him like he was a child. But what's going to happen when you head back to the city, eh? You can't take the dog with you, and he's going to get lonely and sad. How's a dog going to know where you've gone?"

But Pedro loved the dog and wouldn't listen to the farm worker.

Soon it was time to go back, and Pedro's father told him to pack up and get ready to go back to town.

"Please can I take my dog with me?" asked Pedro.

"You must be joking," said his father. "We're not taking that little flea-ridden pup back to the city. It stays right here."

Sadly, the boy climbed onto his horse, and they trotted out of the farm gate. They hadn't gone far when Pedro heard a bark. There was the dog—he had come too. He followed them all the way to the city. Pedro felt proud that it liked him enough to do that, and there was nothing his father could do about it.

When they arrived, Pedro showed the dog an old kennel and put him in there. Then he rushed indoors to take a bath after the long ride. As soon as he had changed, he ran out to see the dog. But instead of running out to meet him and lick him, it held back and snarled.

"What's the matter? It's me. Remember me? Don't be frightened," Pedro said.

But it didn't make any difference. The dog wouldn't be friendly. The next day when Pedro went to the kennel—nothing.

The dog had gone. Pedro felt so miserable. He couldn't understand it. Why had the dog done this? He rushed off to his father.

"Why has my dog gone and left me?"

"I think I know," said his father. "When you came home, you took off your poncho. The dog didn't know who you were. He thought you were a different boy in that fancy city shirt. I tell you what. Next year you can put on your poncho, come with me back to the farm and you'll see, you'll be able to feed him again."

And sure enough, when Pedro went back the next year, there was his dog. When he saw him in that poncho, up he came wagging his tail, and the two of them were friends again.

THE LITTLE GREEN FROG

illustrated by Anita Kunz

Patricia thought that the stories the Indians told were very silly—stories like the one that said children could be turned into little frogs if their mothers leave them. They have fathers to look after them, don't they? she thought. And she saw lots of children with no mother out on the streets, begging. And they never got turned into frogs, did they?

On the way back from school she told Tero what she thought about the Indians' stories. Tero was her best friend. He wanted to talk about other things, but Patricia wouldn't leave the matter alone.

"Can you imagine? Stories like the sun and the moon coming out of a cave, or stuff like all men and women coming out of a cave as well, and that one about the sea where—"

"Oh, forget it, Patricia," said Tero, "I'm hungry, and it doesn't really matter anyway."

Tero turned off into his house, and Patricia walked on. When she was standing by the side of the road, waiting to cross, a huge truck roared by. It was loaded with trees, massive trunks just cut down from the forest. Some of them still had branches and leaves on them. As it passed Patricia, the back wheels of the truck hit a pothole and jolted its load. A soft green thing fell from a branch, almost onto her feet. Patricia jumped. She took a step back and then, slowly, she moved closer to see what had fallen off the truck—it was a little green frog.

She stared at it. There it sat, a dull, ashy green color. She could see its bones through the green skin, and its eyes were half-closed. It sat very still, and close to the ground. It was still breathing, but Patricia saw that it wouldn't last long out here where it could be crushed and where the sun would dry it out.

She bent down to pick it up but stopped sharply. A voice seemed to come from the frog saying, "Oh dear, oh dear."

Patricia stood up again and started to run off, but then she stopped. She thought, this is silly, frogs can't talk, but...but I heard it. She crouched down again and reached out her hand.

"Don't touch me. Don't kill me," said the frog.

Before she knew it, Patricia was talking back.

"Why can't I touch you?"

"Don't kill me," said the frog.

"I'm not going to kill you," said Patricia. "I only want to move you to a cool place and keep you from being squashed."

The little frog lifted its head up and opened its eyes more. It had greenish yellow eyes with beautiful spots that changed color in the light.

"Well, all right," said the frog. "Thank you."

Patricia looked for a cool place by the side of the road but could not see one. Then she had her idea. She'd take it and put it on the grass that grew at the side of her house. She only hoped that her uncle who lived in her house did not see it because he was a gruff, moody sort of

person and might tell her off and throw the little frog onto the road.

So, when she got back to the house, she put the little frog on the cool grass next to one of the walls. Then very quietly, she said, "I'll be back, don't move."

She went into the house, trying to act as if nothing had happened. But there was nobody at home except her older brother Ico. He hadn't gone to school that day because of a cold. She thought of telling him about the little frog but held back. He was too much of a chatterbox to keep such a secret.

She felt she had to tell someone about what she had found, but who? Her uncle? No way! Isabelita, who looked after Ico and her when their parents were away? No, she would think it was black magic. Tero? Maybe.

Patricia went into the kitchen. There was some food for her on the table, but she wasn't hungry. Hungry? The little green frog must be hungry…and thirsty. She could take her dinner to the frog, but then—what do frogs eat?

Patricia jumped. She was talking to herself and didn't see Ico come in.

"What did you say?" he said.

"Nothing," Patricia said.

But she needed to tell him. Perhaps she *could* trust Ico with her secret, even though he was a chatterbox.

"Ico?"

"Mmm."

"What do frogs eat?"

"Why do you ask?" said Ico.

"No, no nothing."

The silence made Patricia tell him.

"Look Ico, I found a little green frog that talks, out on the road. It fell off a truck right at my feet," she said all in a rush.

Ico looked at her, astounded. He knew that his sister liked to make things up sometimes, but this time she looked so serious.

"Come and see," she said.

Patricia took Ico out of the house to the cool grass by the wall. The little green frog was still there. It looked as if it were asleep.

"Look," said Patricia.

"Tell it to talk," said Ico.

"No, it's asleep. Let's get it some food for when it wakes up."

"No," said the frog.

Ico's eyes nearly popped out. He was going to run away, but Patricia grabbed him by the shirt.

"Wait!" she said.

Ico didn't say a word.

"Don't bother with the food," said the frog. "Just bring me some water. I'm thirsty."

"Get some water," said Patricia to Ico. But he was so frightened he couldn't move. Patricia had to go to the tap herself.

"Don't be afraid," said the frog to Ico. "After I've had a drink, I'll tell you my story."

Patricia brought some water in a little china saucer. The little frog drank slowly. Its skin came back to life and looked much brighter and greener. The children could see that it was feeling better.

"Let's take it indoors," said Ico. Patricia and the frog agreed. They put it on a cotton cloth on the table next to Beto the goldfish, who swam back and forth in a glass bowl. The frog was about to start telling its story when Patricia asked it to wait just a little longer. She wanted her friend Tero to hear the story too, and she ran off and got him. All was ready for the frog to begin:

Hundreds of years ago, the first men and women on this island lived in two caves. One cave was called Cacibajagua. The people in that cave, my people, only came out at night. They were afraid of the sun because they thought it would turn them into trees, stones, or animals.

One night the chief sent his brother out to catch fish, but he didn't get back to the cave in time. He was surprised by the sun and turned into a swallow. The chief was so upset that he left cave Cacibajagua. He took all the women and children with him to the bank of a big river. Then he made the mothers leave their children on the river bank. The children cried out "Toa, toa," which is what children call their mothers in our language.

Morning came, and when the sun rose, it turned all the children into frogs. There they sat, crying helplessly. Then the spirit of the water rose out of the river, her body as clear as glass. The frogs told her what had happened, and she felt sorry for them. She said, "I cannot change what has happened to you, but I can ask the great goddess to let you go back to Cacibajagua when you die. As long as you die a natural death, you will turn back into children and live in the cave for the rest of the time."

The little frogs thanked the water spirit.

Before they left, she gave them each a long, thin gold medal, the kind our people used to wear on their foreheads. "Each of you must have one of these with you when you die;" she said, "otherwise you won't turn back into children." And the water spirit disappeared into the river.

The frogs put the medals in their mouths and made their way up the great river to one of the little streams that flowed into it. There they found a nice cool place, where there was lots of food, since from now on they would have to eat insects and grubs.

Many years passed. The frogs saw the people of the island working together like brothers and sisters, without harming nature, only taking what they needed to live; fruit from the trees, fish from the river, and what animals they needed but no more. And when the frogs died a natural death, they went back to cave Cacibajagua and turned into children.

But one day, other people came to the island. They got rid of the peaceful people, and in no time at all they began to damage the forest and the rivers and the animals. The sons and daughters of the first little frogs found it more and more difficult to find good places to live, and they began to move away. The world was changing, and they felt that the rain gods had abandoned them.

(The little green frog paused. He looked tired now, but sipped some water and carried on.)

The last of my people lived in a little pine forest that was cool and green. But a few days ago the men and machines came and chopped down all the trees. A lot of my brothers and sisters were squashed and died and could not get back to Cacibajagua. Maybe there are others who have been saved like me. But without water they will die of thirst and that is not a natural death. They won't be able to return to the cave—and you know what that means: no more children.

A greenish light began to surround the little frog. The light spread until it filled the whole room. Suddenly the little green frog opened its eyes very wide and shouted happily like a child "Toa!"

The light made the three children sleepy. They fell back on the bed where they had been sitting, listening. They didn't see the little green frog turn into a naked short-haired boy and disappear.

Isabelita came into the room and turned on the light.

"Ico, Patricia, come and have your tea. Tero! You're here? Your mother is looking for you everywhere."

The three of them looked at each other, puzzled. Then, almost at the same time, they rushed to the table. Beto was waving his colored fins around. Beside the fish bowl was a white cotton cloth and on it, a little flat golden thing—the little green frog's medal.

THE GREEDY FATHER

illustrated by David Sim

Long ago there came a terrible time in southern Africa. There was a severe famine. People and animals had nothing to eat. Many were starving and dying. Water was scarce; the rivers were drying up. Only pools of stagnant water could be seen where before rivers flowed.

At this time there lived a man called Temdere and his wife and three children.

"Why do you just sit there, my husband?" said Anesu, his wife. "Other fathers are out hunting and looking for food."

"What about you?" said Temdere. "Why don't you go out hunting for food? I hear that your parents have plenty in their hut. I'm not going hunting. I'm tired."

These arguments and quarrels happened every day. Food was getting scarcer and scarcer. Rain didn't come. People stopped going to the fields, and instead the men went to faraway forests to hunt for skinny, dying animals and the little honey they could find.

Finally, after weeks of quarreling,

Temdere decided to go to the forests too. He tried to chase animals, but he had no dogs to help him. One day as he was walking home with nothing at all, he heard a honey bird sing. He followed it and came across a huge bees' nest. "At last," he thought, "a bit of luck." And there and then he decided he would have the biggest share of the honey for himself. But how?

He rushed home and got himself a gourd—the fruit of a plant that when it dries out makes a perfect water pot. Then he hurried back to the nest, made a fire to drive off the bees, and sat down and ate honey and more honey till he could eat no more. He was so pleased with himself. Now, he filled the gourd with honey and dug a hole in the ground, put the gourd in the hole and covered it up. Then he slipped a reed into the gourd with just the top sticking out, like a straw. And he left for home. He arrived back with nothing more than five locusts that he caught on the way home.

"The forests have nothing, my wife," he

said. "I've tried my best, but I have failed."

Anesu was furious with him.

"I believe that I am doomed, my dear. The spirits of my ancestors do not protect me as they should, and they are letting witches cast spells on me so that we will all die."

"Nonsense and rubbish," said Anesu, but there was nothing that could be done. She divided the little food there was, but Temdere made a great show of refusing his share.

"No, no, you eat. I am nothing but a worthless fool. I will die and you must live. If I can't hunt and find food for you, then it is right that I should die first. The children must come first."

The following day he went to his hideaway spot and sucked more honey out of the gourd. He also managed to find an injured antelope. He killed it, roasted it over a fire, and ate it there and then.

That night he came home with just a tiny bit of meat, saying, "Today for the first time, I had some luck. I caught an antelope, but some other hunters came and stole most of it off me. Give it to the children, my dear, for they must live."

And so it went on, day after day. Temdere went out, ate, came back with little or nothing, and refused to eat. Anesu started getting suspicious. "Something's going on here," she thought. "Tomorrow I'll follow him and see what he does."

The next day, off went Temdere to his hideaway and started sucking his honey out of the gourd. Anesu watched from behind a bush. Then Temdere lay down and went to sleep. Anesu crept out and

saw it all: the reed, the gourd, the honey. So she sucked out some and took it back for her children.

Later Temdere went back to his feeding spot. He didn't know that some of the honey had gone. That night he came home with two tiny little birds.

"It's all I could catch today, my dear. People are bewitching me, and I can't fend off their evil spirits. There, take them. I won't eat again tonight."

"Very strange, husband, very strange," said Anesu. "Every night you come here, and refuse food. Don't you like the way I cook?"

"Oh, no, my dear. I love the way you cook. I do it out of pity for you and the children."

"How kind of you," said Anesu, "but there is one thing that bothers me. How come we eat and get thinner, and you don't eat and get fatter?"

"Water," said Temdere, "I drink water.

It's a very good medicine when there is a famine."

"Ah, I see," said Anesu. "Well, listen to me. In the morning, I would like you to go and visit my parents. I think they have enough food to give us some."

Temdere didn't really like this idea, but he could hardly say he wouldn't go, and so the next morning off he went. On the way there, he visited the honey gourd, had a drink, put some more honey in it, and walked on to his wife's parents. They had prepared food for him, and he ate like a madman.

"How are the children and your wife?" said his father-in-law.

"Not too good," said Temdere.

He spent two days there, eating, resting, eating, and resting some more. On the third day he left for home.

Each day at home, Anesu and her children went to the gourd to eat honey. But on the third day, she went to the hideaway, took the honey away, and filled the place with earth.

Meanwhile, Temdere came home with a little dried meat that Anesu cooked. As usual, he refused it, for this time he really was full from the good food Anesu's parents had given him.

The following day, Temdere headed for the hideaway. When he got there, he was furious.

"Who has discovered my secret?" he asked. "If I catch him, I'll kill him. It's somebody who's jealous of me. I was stung by bees three times trying to get this honey, and now this happens! Now what will I say when I get home and my wife cooks something? I won't be able to say, 'No, you eat it.' I'll be starving hungry."

"My husband, why are you moaning?"

What was that voice?

"It's me, Anesu."

He turned around and saw her and stood there, speechless. Then he fell to the ground, still as a stone.

"Well, well, well, husband. This is what it's come to. Do you know who stole your honey? It was me and the children. Do you want to know why? Look at your children. They are nothing but skin and bone. You are the cruelest, greediest person I have ever known."

"Forgive me, Anesu, forgive me. I know I have done wrong," said Temdere.

Anesu looked at him lying there.

"Come home with us. And tonight like all other nights I will offer you some food and you can refuse it."

She turned and took her children home with her, while Temdere stumbled along behind.

After this, Temdere tried harder. He managed to get hold of some dogs to help him hunt. At first, Anesu used to follow him to make sure that he wasn't cheating on them again, but no, he seemed to change for the better. And the whole family survived that terrible time, thanks to Anesu.

THE PAINTER AND THE JUDGE

illustrated by Satoshi Kitamura

Once there was a judge who was very mean. Everyone knew that to get him to listen to you, you had to go to him secretly and give him huge amounts of money. And even then he might just take the money and still not give you a fair hearing. People often felt that he had cheated them.

One day the judge heard there was a painter in town who could paint the most wonderful pictures. The judge found the man and gave him a roll of white paper to get working on.

"Paint me a beautiful picture," said the judge.

At first the painter didn't want to. He knew how mean the judge was and said to himself, "I might do a lot of work on this painting and end up not getting paid."

"I'm very busy at the moment," he said. "I just don't have the time."

But the judge begged him, saying, "I shall put it up in a place where all the most important people in town will see it."

In the end the painter said he would do a picture for the judge.

The next day, he came to the judge's house with the roll of paper.

"Wise One, I have finished the painting."

The judge was delighted, but when he unrolled the paper, he couldn't see any picture on it. Instead, there were a few words: "Cows on Grass."

The judge stared at the blank piece of paper.

"But where's the grass?" he said.

"The cows have eaten it," answered the painter.

"But then where are the cows?" said the judge.

"Well," said the painter, "seeing as they'd eaten all the grass, there wasn't much point in them hanging around any longer, was there? So they left."

A STORY FOR A PRINCESS

illustrated by Norman Messenger

Long, long ago, in a country now called Iran, there lived a king who was unbelievably rich. He lived in the most magnificent palace you could imagine, but strangely he and his family were hardly ever seen in public. People said that the queen had had a baby girl many years before who would now be a princess, but no one had ever seen her. It was all very mysterious.

One day the king's chief minister pinned a notice to the wall of the palace:

"I, the king, announce today that I have a daughter who is as kind as she is beautiful. This royal princess has now reached the age when she should marry. I hereby declare that I shall give her hand in marriage to any man who can tell me a story that I think is a lie from beginning to end."

The challenge seemed to be easy, and so men flocked from the farthest corners of the kingdom to try their luck. Yet, somehow, each one came out of the palace minutes later very disappointed.

And so the next man went in and bowed to the king. "Once upon a time—"

"Out! Get out!" shouted the king. "Any story that begins 'Once upon a time' is no good. Who has lived long enough to say whether it's true or not? It just can't be proved. Send in the next man."

In came the next young man. He fell on his face before the king.

"Arise, tell me your story."

"In the name of Allah—"

"Out! Get out! How can any story that begins with the holy name of Allah be a lie? Get out!"

And so it went on for days and days, until finally, in came a rough-looking young man from a far off village in the mountains. His clothes were torn and dirty and around his waist was a belt from which hung a dirty leather pouch.

He bowed to the king and began:

You know, when my great-grandmother, this was on my father's side, you understand well, when this dear old lady gave birth to my grandfather—that's my father's father—are you following me? Well, anyway, when this happened, I was seven years old. I went off to see the new mother and her baby—that's what we do in our village. I kissed both of them and just as I was leaving, you know what happened? My father's grandmother gave me a present—it was an egg. Very nice of her, I thought. It looked much like any other egg. But you know, as I skipped down the road with it, I could feel it getting bigger and bigger in my hands till in the end I couldn't hold on to it any longer. It just fell out of my hands and fell, *splat*, onto the ground. And it broke open and out stepped a giant rooster.

"Get on my back, and I'll carry you home!" it said to me.

So I climbed onto its back and held on tight around its neck. Off we went.

Well, we hadn't gone very far when I realized we weren't going the usual way home. We were going past orange trees with oranges the size of melons, then on past a pool with water lilies that shone like stars. As I bent down to have a closer look, my foot knocked against the rooster's neck and right away a big hole appeared in the skin, and blood started pouring out. But the rooster didn't seem to mind at all.

"Take a date out of your pouch," he said. "Eat it and keep the stone. The stone will turn to powder. Rub the powder into my wound."

So I did as he told me and after I rubbed the powder in, a palm tree started to grow out of the hole. It grew taller and taller until there were huge bunches of dates hanging down in front of me. Oooh, they looked delicious. I couldn't wait to eat some. So I climbed up the trunk of the palm, stretched out, and picked one. It was so huge, it filled my whole hand—have you ever seen a date as big as that?—and it was sweeter than any honey I had ever tasted. As I bit into it, drops of its delicious juice dripped onto the leaves and as I watched, I saw an ant rush out and catch the droplets in a golden jug. Soon

the jug was overflowing, and the ant hurried along the palm leaf, leaving a trail of honey as it went. I followed the trail and was soon surrounded by an army of ants. Each one carried either a jug of honey or a sesame seed.

At the end of a long, long road, the ant army stopped in front of a mountain of sesame seeds. On top of the mountain was a small ant holding a big stick. With the stick it was knocking the seeds one by one into a huge bowl. Another ant was emptying the golden jugs full of honey into the bowl, one by one, on top of the sesame seeds. Then out of nowhere, a huge golden spoon came down and started stirring up the honey and the sesame seeds, stirring and stirring until a huge dome of sesame and honey rose up in front of me. Then, before I could move, the bowl tipped up toward me, and the sesame and honey mountain poured toward me. I couldn't get out of the way. I was just rooted to the spot, and the whole thing poured right over me. I was trapped.

I felt pretty scared, you can imagine, because there was no way out. But then I felt a little tickle on my hand, and there in the middle of my palm stood a tiny ant.

"Don't be frightened," it said in a tiny voice. "You can easily eat your way out of here."

"I don't feel hungry," I said.

"Too bad," said the ant, "Just begin."

So I started to eat my way out of there, and it wasn't long before I had eaten a hole big enough to crawl through. To tell the truth, I felt a little sick. Well, wouldn't

you—eating all that honey and sesame seed?

I was just about to clean myself off—my clothes were very sticky—when:

"Here, over here! Remember me?"

It was the ant. It was standing on my wrist, holding two shiny white sesame seeds.

"Listen, you must plant these seeds right now, quick before the General notices they're missing. He counts every one, you know."

I began right away and planted them.

By now I was feeling very tired, so I lay down to sleep. When I woke up, I was in the middle of fields and fields of sesame.

"Come on," said someone, "get up, it's time to gather in the harvest."

It was the ant again. So we began to collect the ripe sesame seeds. The more we gathered, the more there seemed to be.

"What are we going to do with all these sesame seeds?" I said.

"Don't ask silly questions," said the ant. "Just drop one on the ground and tread on it."

I did and a huge river of oil flowed out of the seed. Soon I was the richest, most famous oil merchant in the whole kingdom.

I should have been the happiest man in the world, but somehow, every night, when I went to bed and tried to get to sleep, all I could see in front of my eyes, open or closed, were sesame seeds.

And one night I could even see the ant general. He was huge and fierce, and he bellowed at me: "YOU HAVE STOLEN TWO OF MY SESAME SEEDS!"

"Don't kill me," I cried. "Spare me, mercy, mercy," and I woke up.

"Enough is enough," I said to myself. "I've had enough of sesame seeds. There must be something else I can grow." And I went out in my garden to think about it. I put my hand into my pouch and yes, of course, there were a few sesame seeds left in there and I threw them on the ground.

These grew into huge sunflowers. They were the biggest sunflowers I had ever seen. Their petals were made of gold. And the flowers just kept growing and growing. I went into my house and got a ladder, propped it up against a stalk, and started climbing.

As I climbed, a horrible thought came into my mind...sunflowers have big seeds, seeds much bigger than sesame seeds, bigger seeds means more oil...But I couldn't keep myself from climbing and climbing to the top, and just as I got to the petals a great cloud of pollen floated past me. Some went up my nose, and I gave what must have been one of the biggest sneezes the world has ever heard. I sneezed so hard the ground shook, and I went flying through the air. I landed with a great thump in the middle of a crowd of people.

They were reading some kind of notice that said, "I, the king, announce today that I have a daughter who is as kind as she is beautiful. This royal princess has now reached the age when she should marry. I hereby declare that I..."

"Stop, stop!" shouted the king. "You've won. You're the winner. You shall marry my daughter."

Everyone was delighted.

Before he knew what was happening, the princess was brought in wearing a dark veil, and the marriage ceremony began. There was singing and laughing and at long last the time came for the bridegroom to lift the princess's veil. But when he did —horror of horrors—he saw a face uglier and more terrifying than anything he had ever seen in his life. He didn't wait to find out if she was as kind as she was beautiful. He just fled. He took himself out of the door as fast as anyone has ever run. He ran all the way back home to the far off village in the mountains.

Safely back in his father's house, he undid his belt and dropped it on the rough old table. As he put his head in his hands, to bless Allah for his lucky escape, out of the corner of his eye he saw that a date stone, a sesame seed, and a sunflower seed had fallen out of the pouch. And then down his arm onto the table scurried a little ant.

ABOUT THE ARTISTS

WAYNE ANDERSON

Born in 1946 in England, Wayne Anderson received his art degree in 1966. He has illustrated several books for children, and his work has been exhibited in galleries in England and the United States. He has recently started his own company, producing cards, prints, and posters of his own work.

NICOLA BAYLEY

Born in Singapore in 1949, Nicola Bayley studied art at St. Martin's School of Art and the Royal College of Art in England. She produces brilliantly colored miniature illustrations, and lives in southwest London with her husband John, small son Felix, and cat Bella.

LOUISE BRIERLEY

Born in 1958, Louise Brierley studied art at Manchester Polytechnic and the Royal College of Art in England. Her work has been exhibited in several countries, including the United States, Japan, Germany, and England. Her first book for children was published in 1981.

CHRISTOPHER BROWN

A popular illustrator in England for more than ten years, Christopher Brown has had commissions from publishing houses as well as advertising agencies and design groups. His work has been included in many art exhibitions and has won numerous awards.

JOHN BURNINGHAM

Born in 1936, John Burningham studied at the Central School of Art in London. He has illustrated numerous highly-acclaimed picture books and has won the Kate Greenaway Medal (the English equivalent of the Caldecott Medal). He lives with his wife and three children in London.

REG CARTWRIGHT

Without any formal art training, Reg Cartwright entered the advertising world as an art director in 1960. His first children's book, based on one of his posters, won him the Mother Goose Award in England in 1980 as the most promising new children's book illustrator.

CHRISTOPHER CORR

In addition to being exhibited in numerous shows in both England and the United States, Christopher Corr's work has been featured on two BBC television programs. He is best known for his colorful watercolors based on his travels throughout the world, but he also works in other mediums including collage and lithography.

CATHIE FELSTEAD

After receiving her masters degree from the Royal College of Art in England, Cathie Felstead became a free-lance illustrator. She has illustrated record covers and book jackets and has painted ballet sets. This book is the first children's book to which she has contributed interior artwork.

MICHAEL FOREMAN

An illustrator of numerous children's picture books, Michael Foreman has won several major awards, including the Kate Greenaway Medal (the British equivalent of the Caldecott Medal). He is married with three sons and lives in London.

SATOSHI KITAMURA

At one time an advertising and magazine illustrator in Japan, Satoshi Kitamura later turned his interests to children's books. In 1983 he won the Mother Goose Award as the most promising newcomer to the field of children's books in England. He lives in London.

ANITA KUNZ

Born in Toronto, Ontario, in 1956, Anita Kunz has lived and worked there almost all her life, doing free-lance work for advertising agencies and book and magazine publishers, including *The New York Times*, *The Atlantic Monthly*, and *Rolling Stone*. Her paintings have appeared in many group shows internationally, and she has won numerous awards for her work.

JAMES MARSH

Born in 1946 in Yorkshire, England, James Marsh divides his time equally between editorial, advertising, and publishing work. He has written and illustrated two children's books and his paintings are in public and private collections throughout the world.

CLARE MELINSKY

Although she specialized in theater and costume design at college, Clare Melinsky took up block printing with linoleum cuts on fabric upon leaving school. Her technique is self-taught and was developed from studying the work of traditional English block printers. She now works at her home in Scotland, where she lives with her husband and two children.

NORMAN MESSENGER

Before turning to free-lance illustration for magazine and book publishers, Norman Messenger worked in London as an advertising art director. He was the winner of the Red Book Children's Picture Book Award in 1989. He lives in Gloucestershire, England, with his illustrator-painter wife, two sons, and one cat.

HELEN OXENBURY

Born in Ipswich, England, Helen Oxenbury studied theater design at the Central School of Art in London. She turned from working in theater, film, and television while expecting her first child, and has been writing and illustrating acclaimed picture books ever since. She has now illustrated nearly sixty titles. She has won the prestigious Kate Greenaway Medal (the British equivalent of the Caldecott Medal) as well as a Boston Globe-Horn Book Honor Award. She lives in London with her husband and children.

RICHARD PARENT

Working as a free-lance illustrator, Richard Parent most enjoys doing artwork for magazines, theater posters, and book jackets that deal with contemporary social issues. He has done work for various organizations, including Greenpeace and the Canadian Cancer Research Society. Richard Parent lives in Montreal, Canada.

GRAHAM PERCY

Born in New Zealand, Graham Percy moved to England to study graphic design at the Royal College of Art. He is now an illustrator of children's books and lives in London.

AXEL SCHEFFLER

Born in Germany in 1957, Axel Scheffler studied art history at Hamburg University and visual communications at the Bath Academy of Art in England. Since 1985 he has worked as a free-lance illustrator in England and Germany.

DAVID SIM

Born in Glasgow, Scotland, in 1953, David Sim studied graphic design and illustration at the Edinburgh College of Art and Illustration and printmaking at the Royal College of Art in London. Although he is now a part-time teacher he has been working as a free-lance illustrator since 1980.

CHARLOTTE VOAKE

Although she had no formal art training, Charlotte Voake always wanted to be an illustrator. She has illustrated more than ten books for children and won many awards for her work. She lives in Surrey, England, with her husband and daughter.

LOUISE VOCE

Born in England, Louise Voce received both undergraduate and graduate degrees in graphic design. She has illustrated several picture books for children and lives in Liverpool, England.

JANET WOOLLEY

A free-lance illustrator working for a variety of magazines and journals, Janet Woolley studied illustration at the Royal College of Art in London, where she finished her nine years of art training.

ACKNOWLEDGEMENTS

Oxfam, the editor, and the publishers, Candlewick Press, would like to thank all the people and organizations who helped make this book happen:

☐ *Staff in Oxfams in the United Kingdom and Ireland, the United States, Canada, Hong Kong, and in Community Aid Abroad in Australia who submitted suggestions for stories;*

☐ *Field staff and project partners in Africa, Asia, the Caribbean, and Central and South America who sent in stories.*

We especially want to thank the following for particular stories:

☐ *Marieke Clarke, now working on the Asia desk in Oxfam UKI, for suggesting* Mansoor and the Donkey, The Strongest Person in the World, The Four Brothers, *and* Pedro and His Dog, *all of which she had come upon while working on a world story program in the Oxfam Education Department;*

☐ *Michael Butcher, a former Oxfam Field Officer in West Africa, who collected* Why Do Dogs Chase Cars?, *a popular story in the area;*

☐ *The Ticuna Indian people from the Amazon Basin for one of their creation stories,* The Beginning of History, *translated from the Portuguese for Michael Rosen by Gisela Ferreira Pita;*

☐ *Sabita Limbu and Pemkit Lepcha from Nepal, and Gillian Gee of Oxfam's Overseas Division, to whom they told the story, for* Sunkaissa, the Golden Haired Princess;

☐ *Ced Hesse, of the Oxfam Arid Lands Unit in Dakar, Senegal, and Mamadou Karambe from Mali, for* Ears, Eyes, Legs, and Arms;

☐ *The many Oxfam staff who suggested different versions of* Snake, Horse, and Toad;

☐ *Centro Dominicano de Estudios de la Educacion in Santo Domingo for contributing* The Little Green Frog, *and Mary Hanton of the Oxfam UKI Latin America and Caribbean desk for providing a translation;*

☐ *Colettah Chitsike, an Oxfam Rural Development Adviser in the Mulanje District of Malawi, for* The Greedy Father, *a story from her home country of Zimbabwe;*

☐ *The schoolchildren in London who told Michael Rosen their stories; especially Jason, Andrew, Marie, Antony, Ming, Jason, and Dinar.*

About Oxfam

Working for a Fairer World

This collection of stories can open windows into other cultures and lives. With the rapid growth of international travel and worldwide communications the world is shrinking, and we share experiences with more and more people. Through this book we can share stories from other cultures, but there are other experiences that we would probably not choose to share.

Every day, millions of people in many countries go without things we in developed countries take for granted: food, shelter, water, education, health care, and the right to make decisions about our own lives. For many poor people things are getting worse, not better.

Oxfam is helping people break out of their poverty by supporting them in efforts to make changes that will last.

The Early Years

In 1942 the world is at war. Most of Europe is occupied by Nazi forces, and innocent civilians are suffering. In Oxford, England, on 5 October 1942, a group of people form the Oxford Committee for Famine Relief. Its aim: to relieve the suffering of civilians in Greece, and to press for supplies to be allowed through the Allied blockade. The Oxford Committee joins with Famine Relief Committees around the country to lobby British and Allied governments. A trickle of food is allowed into Greece before the war ends, but it is only after liberation in 1944 and the end of the blockade that the trickle becomes a more adequate supply.

The Oxford Committee raises funds and supplies for the Greek Red Cross to support the victims of conflict. Donations come in from appeals to the public, and through a temporary "gift shop."

When peace comes in 1945, the Oxford Committee finds there is still work to do. More than 30 million refugees are moving across the borders of Europe—with no possessions, no homes, and no future. The Oxford Committee (it doesn't change its name to Oxfam for another twenty years) raises money and collects clothing. The money pays for food and shelter, and the clothing is shipped to frightened and shattered families across Europe, even including Germany.

The Oxfam Committee doesn't disband. It continues to organize relief for refugees from conflict and for victims of natural disasters. In 1965 the charity adopts its telegram name, Oxfam, as its registered name. It expands its activities and its vision and continues on the road to becoming the Oxfam we know today.

Oxfam Overseas

Oxfam, which started life in war-torn Europe, now works in seventy-seven countries and supports over 2,000 long-term development projects. Much of its work is in places where conflict makes life almost unsupportable for innocent victims. A common theme through Oxfam's development is the commitment to humanitarian help for people, irrespective of religious or political boundaries.

Oxfam still carries out much emergency work but is also committed to the wider and more lasting relief of suffering. It works alongside the very poorest people, supporting them in their efforts to break free of sickness, illiteracy, powerlessness, and poverty, and arguing against the injustice that causes them. Through its work, Oxfam helps to challenge the exploitation and injustice that keeps people poor.

Oxfam staff keeps in regular contact with project partners, giving support and advice and ensuring that grants are well spent. Many self-help projects are small scale, needing minimal financial support. Many Oxfam grants are for under $5,000 but the impact of these small sums is considerable. After decades of experience Oxfam knows that the projects most likely to succeed are those in which people are working for their own development.

The International Oxfam Family

Gradually, the approach to development work pioneered by the first Oxfam has spread to other countries around the world. In 1953, Community Aid Abroad started in Melbourne, Australia, to raise funds to alleviate hunger in India. Today CAA works in twenty-five countries and is Australia's oldest independent overseas aid and development agency. In 1963, Oxfam Belgium began after a group of friends had seen work supported by Oxfam in Rwanda. Over 150 permanent shop-based groups now support the overseas work of the agency. In the same year, Oxfam Canada was founded. Maximizing the role and involvement of volunteers, it established regional and national volunteer boards. After considerable growth, Oxfam Canada now has eleven offices in Canada and three overseas. In 1970, concerned individuals in the United States founded Oxfam America to respond to the floods that year in Bangladesh. To maintain its independence, they decided from the start not to solicit or accept government funds. The last five years have seen the establishment of eight overseas offices, along with the development of regional volunteer committees within the U.S. In 1973, with the support of Oxfam Canada, Oxfam Quebec was formed. It recently assumed a key role in the development of the *Montreal Charter*, which defines access to drinking water as a basic human right. The newest addition to the Oxfam family, Oxfam Hong Kong, joined the group in 1986 following successful fundraising efforts during the 1984-85 Ethiopian famine.

Although all these organizations function autonomously, they strive to work collaboratively with overseas project partners. Most have overseas offices as well as decentralized regional offices in their own countries. Most also raise funds through the catalog sale of crafts produced in self-help development projects where Oxfam supplies marketing and training support. All have education programs aimed at telling potential supporters about the problems faced by those in developing countries.

The 50th anniversary of the founding of the first Oxfam, in Oxford, England, has provided an opportunity for all seven Oxfams to work more closely together, fostering joint fundraising initiatives, campaigns,... and this book. All seven organizations look forward to further cooperation and the addition of new members to the international Oxfam family.

OXFAM
WORKING FOR A FAIRER WORLD

Since 1942, Oxfam has provided people with support regardless of their race, color, gender, politics, or religion. Oxfam supports projects that try to achieve certain goals. They should:

☐ meet an important need of the local community.

☐ have a clear set of goals from the beginning.

☐ work with low-income groups, both rural and urban.

☐ build self-reliance by improving long-term food security.

☐ increase economic and social equity.

☐ strengthen people's capacity to change the social and economic conditions that keep them poor.

☐ encourage other development efforts locally and regionally.

Oxfam can only provide this support with help from you. By buying this book you have already contributed, since the royalty benefits Oxfam's partners.

There are other ways that you can work with Oxfam for a fairer world. You can:

☐ make a regular monthly gift, which ensures that Oxfam's partners will have consistent and reliable support.

☐ organize a special event in your community, church, or workplace.

☐ join a local volunteer committee to help raise funds and awareness.

☐ take part in campaigns to bring the voice of Oxfam's project partners to members of government responsible for aid policy.

☐ encourage your workplace to make a corporate gift or to match your personal gift to Oxfam.

☐ give what you can when you can.

To learn more about Oxfam contact us in:

AUSTRALIA
Community Aid Abroad
156 George Street
Fitzroy, Victoria
3065
Tel. 3-419-7111

BELGIUM
Oxfam Belgique
39 Rue de Conseil
1050 Bruxelles
Tel. 2-512-9990

CANADA
Oxfam Canada
251 Laurier
Avenue W.
Room 301
Ottawa
Ontario K1P 5J6
Tel. 613-237-5236

Oxfam Quebec
169 Rue St. Paul Est
Montreal 127
Quebec H2Y 1G8
Tel. 514-866-1773

HONG KONG
Oxfam
Ground Floor
3B, June Garden
28 Tung Chau St.
Tai Kok Tsui
Kowloon
Tel. 3-916305

IRELAND
Oxfam
202 Lower
Rathmines Road
Dublin 6
Tel. 1-972195

UNITED KINGDOM
Oxfam
274 Banbury Road
Oxford OX2 7DZ
Tel. 0865-311311

UNITED STATES
Oxfam America
115 Broadway
Boston MA 02116
Tel. 617-482-1211

Most of the stories in this book were collected by Oxfam staff who heard them first from people they work with in different countries around the world. Here are some examples of projects funded in countries mentioned in the book.

OXFAM HAS WORKED IN:

BANGLADESH, providing women flood survivors with supplies and credit to buy and grow food.

BOLIVIA, supporting the efforts of indigenous groups to claim ownership of land they have farmed for centuries.

BOTSWANA, developing agricultural training projects as part of the "Freedom from Hunger Campaign" in the 1960s.

BRAZIL, supporting organizations representing the rights of Indian peoples of the Amazon Basin.

THE DOMINICAN REPUBLIC, encouraging the development of local markets and literacy programs.

GREECE, where the first Oxfam famine relief grant was made in 1943 and where in 1948, the first project grant was made to The Domestic Training College for Girls in Salonika.

INDIA, assisting women artisans to develop cooperatives and sell their work.

INDONESIA, where many of the goods sold in Oxfam catalogs are produced.

JAMAICA, where several Oxfam-supported street theater groups help with popular education.

MALI, where recent funding has supported agricultural work providing clean water and health care.

MOZAMBIQUE, improving the water supply for the war-displaced.

SUDAN, providing boats, nets, and transportation to market for war-displaced fisherfolk and their families.

VIETNAM, supplying basic equipment to village-level health clinics.

In total, the combined Oxfam family of organizations currently works in seventy-seven different countries.